# Eureka Point

## By

## Betty Ann Harris

This is a work of fiction. Names, characters, places, and incidents are products of the author's imagination or are used fictitiously and are not to be construed as real. Any resemblance to actual events, locales, organizations, or persons, living or dead, is entirely coincidental. All references to real places, people, or events are coincidental, and if not coincidental, are used fictitiously. All trademarks, service marks, registered trademarks, and registered service marks are the property of their respective owners and are used herein for identification purposes only.

**Eureka Point by Betty Ann Harris**

Red Rose™ Publishing
Publishing with a touch of Class! ™
The symbol of the Red Rose and Red Rose is a trademark of Red Rose™ Publishing

Copyright© 2007 Betty Ann Harris
ISBN: 978-1-60435-970-1
ISBN: 1-60435-970-6
Cover Artist: Red Rose™ Publishing
Editor: Melissa Glisan

All rights reserved. No part of this book may be used or reproduced electronically or in print without written permission, except in the case of brief quotations embodied in reviews.

Red Rose™ Publishing
www.redrosepublishing.com
Forestport, NY 13338

Thank you for purchasing a book from Red Rose™ Publishing where publishing comes with a touch of Class!

## Dedication:

*To all the friends and family who supported me, but most especially to my Dad, who taught me to work hard to achieve my dreams and to never give up.*

I hope you enjoy my first book, Eureka Point.

Betty Ann Harris

# Chapter One

KATIE, LONG ISLAND, NEW YORK

The day had gone exceptionally well. The decorating assignment I'd been working on for the last five months had finally come to completion and my client was delighted with the outcome.

Driftwood, Carly's Long Island cottage, turned out to be one of the best decorating jobs I have ever completed and I was extremely happy about that. Carly was such a nice person and over the five months I worked on the assignment we became good friends. *Elegant Interiors Magazine* was featuring Driftwood in their next issue. It would be the first time one of my interior designs would be appearing in the prestigious magazine. It would definitely serve as a boost to my already lucrative career. I was happy and excited and in the mood to celebrate.

With that assignment complete, I planned to take several weeks off and travel to Bermuda with Craig for some well-deserved rest, relaxation, and perhaps, some romance. Lying on a beautiful beach with my toes in the sand while sipping a pina colada seemed like the perfect payoff for the months of hard work I had put into the assignment. Excited, I couldn't wait to get home and celebrate with Craig. Carly had thoughtfully arranged for her chauffeur to drive me home. I sat back in the limo and enjoyed the ride, admiring the beautiful landscape along the Long Island coastline. A bit later, once it came into view, I marveled at the sheer magnitude of the New York City skyline off in the distance.

My career was on course, I had a close circle of friends and my parents were healthy, happy and enjoying their retirement years. For the most part I was content. Yet I couldn't shake the feeling of something not being quite right, like a nagging thorn festering just under the surface of my skin. Recently I felt a detachment from Craig, whose priority was his restaurant business, which had been occupying more and more of his time. Perhaps this trip to Bermuda would help to bring us closer together and re-ignite the fire in our relationship. I had been missing that fall-in-love type of enthusiasm Craig and I shared when we first began dating. The passion had lasted into our marriage but had slowly died off. I knew it was somewhat common for married couples to occasionally fall into a dull routine after a few years, but I didn't want that to happen to us. I refused to allow Craig and I to drift apart. My priority was to save my marriage, to get back the love and passion, and I hoped it would be his as well.

As the limousine pulled into the driveway, I grew apprehensive. The house was dark and appeared deserted.

I gladly accepted the driver's kind offer to escort me inside. Once inside, I switched on the light in the foyer and disarmed the security system. Thanking the driver for his assistance, I handed him a twenty-dollar bill. He thanked me courteously, tipped his hat, and left quietly, closing the front door. And there I stood, alone. I went over to the front window, slightly pulled back the curtain and watched the limo drive off. I wondered where Craig was this time. Perhaps he was just late, although he hadn't called or left a message on the answering machine as he usually would.

After switching on the living room lamp, I sat on the sofa and kicked off my shoes. I noticed an envelope propped up on the mantel. Curious, I went over to the fireplace and hesitantly picked it up. My name was written on the front in Craig's handwriting. I braced myself for disappointment. My instincts were right on target as I read the note:

*Dearest Kate,*

*I'm sure congratulations are in order. I know you had your heart set on Bermuda. Unfortunately we will have to delay our trip. One of my largest restaurant suppliers in California is having a problem that I need to take care of or it could cause serious problems for me. I had to fly out this afternoon. If I get a chance I'll give you a call sometime tomorrow.*

*Love, Craig.*

"Of course!" I said aloud as I recalled all the times Craig and I were supposed to take a vacation together or celebrate over a romantic dinner and he had gotten called away. Perturbed and let down, I rationalized that this is the price one pays for success. I was very seriously beginning to wonder if it was worth it. What good is success if you don't have the time to enjoy the fruits of your labor? It bothered me that it didn't bother Craig. He seemed to thrive on the stress of it all. Or maybe he didn't feel the stress, just the thrill of being a success in business. It seemed like he was out to prove something to the world.

I've been through this kind of thing before and decided I wasn't going to let Craig's absence ruin my sense of accomplishment or my desire to celebrate. I returned to the kitchen and opened the refrigerator. I grabbed the bottle of champagne I had left in there to chill just that morning. I wrapped a kitchen towel around the bottle and tilted it, pointing it away from my face, as I had seen Craig do many times before. As I carefully opened the bottle, the top flew off, popping loudly, and champagne erupted out, flowing down the sides. I poured myself a glass, took it into the living room, put on my favorite music, and toasted myself.

It was late October and although the weather had been unseasonably warm, tonight there was a definite chill in the air, so I lit a fire in the fireplace and stood in front of it, allowing the warmth of the flames to permeate through my body. I returned to the sofa and sipped the champagne, feeling the rush go through my limbs. Warmth followed, mellowing me as my mind wandered, taking me back to my high school days and my friends from the neighborhood in Philadelphia. I wondered what Jeannine was up to these days and decided I would try to find her and give her a call sometime soon. I missed those good old days and wished times hadn't changed so drastically.

After two glasses of champagne I decided it would probably be a good idea for me to eat something or I would end up sloshed. Last night I had made French beef stew in burgundy wine sauce for the two of us. Craig had forgotten to tell me he had a dinner engagement and his portion had been left over, so I heated that up now for dinner. I've always enjoyed cooking but lacked the enthusiasm to prepare a meal for just myself.

While I ate, I gazed out of the dining room window to watch the full autumn moon rising in the dark sky like a huge golden lantern with feathery clouds flying past it. The scene was dramatic and magical and stirred something deep within me. I had a sense of longing, but exactly what for, I did not know. The moon always fascinated me and I was hypnotized by its beauty and allured by its power. A full moon often made me feel romantic and nostalgic. *What a waste, to be alone on such a wonderful evening.* While I stared at that full gorgeous moon, a strange sensation came over me, as if the moon beseeched me, called to me, tried to tell me something. Or maybe it was the champagne affecting me.

As if reading my mind, a huge, dark cloud passed in front of the moon, removing it from sight. I wondered if that was an omen of some kind, when suddenly, and as quickly as it had disappeared from view, the moon returned and cast a silvery glow into the darkened room. It settled on me, like a searchlight singling me out.

"What do you want moon?" I asked aloud.

*Yes, too much champagne* I guessed. I was now talking to the moon.

I finished my dinner, cleaned up the dishes and spent the rest of the evening sitting in front of the fireplace. My eyelids grew so heavy that I could no longer keep my eyes open, so I dragged myself upstairs to bed. As tired as I had been, I laid there, snuggled under the covers, unable to sleep. I had a sense of impending doom but rationalized that it was just my imagination.

In the very early morning hours, my tired body finally won and at last I fell asleep. I had a strange dream about being lost in the middle of the deep and dark woods on a miserable and gloomy night. A mist hung around my feet, the rain poured down, soaking me, and I was cold and shivering with fright. And then the clouds parted and a bright, full moon lit my path, helping me to find my way home. It was a house that was not familiar to me but one where I felt I belonged. I stepped inside and warmed myself in front of the fire. Strong but gentle hands came from behind me and rested comfortingly upon my shoulders and I felt safe, warm and content. Then I awoke, greeted by the bright morning sun as it cheerfully streamed in my window.

Craig returned from his trip a week later with a nice tan and in an exceptionally good mood. He never mentioned the business problem he had to take care of, never asked about the decorating job I had completed, nor spoke about our cancelled trip to Bermuda. Neither did I.

Hurt and feeling unappreciated at home, I plunged into my work, completing another decorating job for a wealthy client in East Hampton. Craig was rarely home for dinner and seemed anxious and disinterested when he was there. I tried to talk to him about his disinterest in our marriage, or anything else other than his business, for that matter. He always gave me the same answer – that he was under a lot of stress and did not want to discuss it at that point.

I gave him his space and time and hoped it was just a phase. But as time went on he got irritated and angry if I so much as looked at him in the wrong way. I felt like Craig was holding back and keeping secrets. So, like a cat with her nose out of joint, I kept my distance. It was not in my nature to stir up an angry brew and I usually shied away from confrontations. But I could not shake the sensation that something was wrong.

Finishing the job in East Hampton, I drove home one Friday evening and found the house dark and empty again, as was normal these days. Again, I ate dinner alone and fell asleep on the sofa while watching an old movie. I woke the next morning and realized that Craig had never come home. Anxious and furious, I tried to call him on his cell phone but got a recorded message saying his number was no longer in service. Frantic, I called his office but there was no answer there either. When I contacted some of his business associates, I was told that they had not heard from Craig for several days.

I contacted the police and was told I would have to wait at least forty-eight hours before Craig could be considered a missing person. By Sunday evening I was certain that Craig had either left me and his life behind or that he was dead. I stayed up late every night hoping Craig might call or show up with some explanation or excuse as to where he had been, what had happened and why he had not contacted me. That never happened.

When I finally crawled into bed each night, I tossed and turned, unable to fall asleep. My mind kept going over possible scenarios of what might have happened to him. I finally drifted off to sleep at about three am.

I was startled awake Monday morning by the sound of banging on the front door and men yelling, identifying themselves as FBI agents. They demanded that I let them in. I jumped out of bed, scrambled to put on my slippers and robe, ran down the steps, and frantically unlocked the front door. Several agents pushed open the door, almost knocking me over, as they charged in with guns drawn.

Paralyzed with fear I asked, "Oh my God! What is going on?"

"We're looking for Craig Montgomery. Are you his wife?"

"Yes."

"Is he here?"

"No, Craig has not been home for two days. I contacted the police and tried to report his disappearance on Saturday but was told I would have to wait for at least forty-eight hours before he can be declared a missing person. I was going to contact the police again today. I'm very worried. I can't imagine what might have happened to him."

I was in disbelief and shaking like a leaf, and had just inquired if I needed to call my lawyer when Agent John McClintock, an old and dear friend of my father's, walked in and took control of the situation.

The agents searched the house and were satisfied that Craig was not there and felt I was telling them the truth about not knowing where he was. McClintock suggested that he and I go into the kitchen. He asked me if

I would make a pot of coffee, which I did, and then he told me to sit down so we could talk. I pulled out a chair and nervously sat. My hands were shaking so badly I was unable to hold my coffee cup steady. McClintock, in a gesture of concern and support, took my hands in his and told me he had something he needed to tell me. From his behavior and the look on his face, I knew that whatever it was, it wasn't going to be good news.

He told me an unbelievable story about a drug cartel Craig was allegedly involved with. If this was true, Craig had been dealing drugs on a very large scale and involved in one of the largest drug smuggling operations in South America.

I was shaken to my core and thought I had heard the worst when McClintock reminded me that Craig was a wanted fugitive and I could be in real danger. I asked him why I would be in danger; I had nothing to do with any of this. He explained that if this drug lord believed I had information concerning the cartel, Craig's contacts or their operation, he would have me killed. I sat, pondering the mess I found myself in, unable to respond for several minutes. McClintock told me we had no time to waste. He suggested I get dressed that we needed to go downtown to FBI Headquarters.

"I'm not in any legal trouble myself, am I?" I asked, still dazed as I tried to sort this all out in my mind. Yet no matter how hard I tried, I couldn't comprehend this unbelievable turn of events.

"No Katie. But you may be able to answer some questions that might help us find Craig. And we need to protect you from the cartel, and maybe even from Craig himself. I don't think you really know Craig and what he's capable of. Did you know he'd been in a mental institution being treated for a bipolar disorder for almost a year before you met him? We believe he's delusional at best."

I shook my head, this shocking information barely seeping into my confused mind. "But I've been married to him for almost ten years. Sure, he has a bad temper but never seemed actually dangerous or mentally ill to me."

"I believe he came across to you as a certain kind of person to earn your trust, but the truth is, he deceived and used you. He hid things from you Katie. And it's a safe bet to assume he controlled his rage in order to get what he wanted. But we can discuss all this when we get downtown."

McClintock escorted me upstairs and waited while I dressed and grabbed my purse. We returned downstairs, heading into the garage from the kitchen. I retrieved a few things I had left in my car. McClintock whisked me into his car and drove me to FBI Headquarters downtown. I was in a total state of shock and disbelief. Could this really be happening?

## Chapter Two

TOM, NORTHERN CALIFORNIA

I answered by cell phone quickly, knowing from the ring-tone it was my good friend John McClintock from FBI Headquarters in New York City. "Hey John, what's up?"

"This is top secret Tom. I have a woman here who I'm going to be sending to you. Please be especially nice to this one, okay? I'll consider it a personal favor."

"So what's so special about this woman?"

"I've known her family for a long time she's like a daughter to me. In a nutshell, her psychotic husband is now on our most-wanted list for drug trafficking and selling big time. He's involved with a Costa Rican cartel and they may think she knows too much."

"How much does she know?"

"She knows nothing about any aspect of the cartel or her husband's involvement in it. She's in a total state of shock."

"Okay, can you give me the details of her arrival?"

"Her new identity name will be Elizabeth Harrison. Use the password 'unicorn' and meet her at the Southwestern Airlines terminal, gate six at eleven-forty-five tomorrow morning. Whatever you do, don't be late. I sent her photo to your cell phone so you'll know who she is. And by the way, she's a sweetheart and extremely attractive."

"Well that'll be a nice change from the usual."

"I could have sent her to Quigley in Seattle, but I told her you were the best at this type of thing and that you were a personal friend of mine. Besides, I'm afraid old Quigley would be so starry-eyed he wouldn't be able to be effective. You can thank me later. You owe me," he added, chuckling.

"Remember Sicilian Sam? If she turns out to be twice the angel you say she is, then we'll be even."

McClintock laughed. "Seriously Tom, be careful and stay close. This cartel has a very nasty reputation and her husband is deranged enough to be dangerous. Watch your back."

I'd studied her picture on my cell phone screen. There was something about her that really appealed to me. Nothing I could put my finger on; just a feeling I had. Yes, she was very attractive, and hopefully she would be as nice as John McClintock claimed she was, which would make my job a lot easier.

Let's see—this would be number twenty-three. I had helped twenty-two people start new lives for themselves. It was a good job, but also a demanding, difficult and sometimes dangerous one as well. There were a few people I really liked personally and had gotten attached to, but their situations would change. They returned to their old lives or had to be transferred to another agent and have their identity's changed again for their own safety. It was a bummer when that happened.

But at least I'd made some really good friends over the last few years. That was important, especially after Nancy died. I still missed her and couldn't imagine anyone taking her place in my life. Maybe it would happen some day but I tried not to think about it too much. If something was meant to happen, it would. Love, I'd learned, was a very complicated thing. Besides, I wasn't even sure if I was ready to be romantically involved with anyone again. What if I fell in love with someone and something happened to her, like it had to Nancy? I didn't know if I could handle that kind of loss again. But I knew I didn't want to be alone for the rest of my life.

Nancy had come into my life when I hadn't been looking for someone to share my life with. I was too busy with my career and just having a good time. I think I had actually been avoiding getting close to anyone. I'd thought I would have to give up too much of myself. But after I'd met her, everything changed and I looked at love in a whole new way.

Deep in thought, I was suddenly brought back to reality by the sound of my cell phone ringing. It was McClintock again, acting like an over-protective father.

"Hey, make sure you call me tomorrow and let me know when Elizabeth has arrived, okay?"

"Yes, I will. Stop worrying or your colitis will act up again and then you'll end up in the hospital. I'll talk to you tomorrow, John."

Needing to clear my mind, I drove to Cliffport and parked my car near the lighthouse. I watched the sun plummet into the ocean. The fresh air revived me. It was just after five o'clock, which meant I was officially off the clock for the day. I dreaded going home alone and eating some leftovers from God knows when in front of the tube. The thought of a good meal and a couple glasses of wine at The Inn was much more appealing.

The evening was nice enough for me to leave my car at the lighthouse and walk to The Inn. I took the well-beaten path from the lighthouse to The Inn. I prided myself on the fact that I was in pretty good shape and didn't get winded as I walked the distance to the Inn on an incline. Working out everyday had definitely paid off.

The Inn was all but deserted, a bit early for the winery snobs. I was seated at my usual table, one with a great view of the cliffs and ocean beyond. The staff knew me well and everyone was friendly. I had a glass of wine in front of me before I even asked for it, and Kelly, my waitress, who was young enough to be my daughter, always joked with me. She knew I was involved with the FBI but not exactly what my job with the Bureau was.

"Catch any gangsters recently, Mr. Owens?" she teased.

"No dear, but I did catch a big bass when I went deep sea fishing last weekend. Does that count?"

"It'll do, I guess. What did you do with it? Let it go, I hope."

"Don't worry your little head, Kelly. I always let them go. I fish just for the sport of it."

"That's good. Do you have a boat?"

"No, but I have a buddy in the coast guard who has his own boat, down near Pacifico."

"Sounds like fun. So, should I put you down for the special tonight?"

"Of course, so long as it's not deep sea bass."

"Oh, you are such a joker. I bet after all this time you know what every special is for every day of the week, don't you?"

"Yeah, you can put me down for the special."

Tonight was Tuesday and the special was lobster bisque stew. They served it over rice and it was my favorite meal. As I waited for my dinner I sipped the wine and soaked in the atmosphere and the awesome view, which I never grew tired of admiring. The moonlight shimmered on the water and the lighthouse beacon pierced the darkness. After my dinner arrived I ate slowly, savoring every bite. Kelly brought me another glass of wine. I was in no hurry to finish or to go home.

Steve, an acquaintance of mine, and the piano player for a local band, walked into the restaurant and bought me a brandy while I sat at the bar and waited for the rest of his crew. A short while later they sauntered in, taking their time and stopping to converse with some of the locals. I learned to be patient in this environment. People were laid back on this coast. But I liked it here. This was home to me now.

The group was named Indigo and they played a combination of soft rock and smooth jazz. Steve told the audience about their new song, introducing it as *Double Helix*, and explained that Indigo had just recorded and released their first CD.

Their new song was mystical, haunting, and drew me in like a slow vacuum. I found myself fantasizing about another place and time. Mesmerized by the wine, brandy, and *Double Helix*, my mind drifted. I was feeling good and as easy as it would have been for me to stay longer I decided I to call it a night and head back to my car. After all, I had a new assignment early the next morning and I didn't want to be suffering with a hangover. Picking up my cell phone, I decided to have another look at Ms. Harrison's picture. I needed to have my wits about me, especially for this assignment, or McClintock would have my head on a platter.

Walking back to the car I kept playing *Double Helix* over and over again in my head. I would have to remember to tell Steve it was a good tune, memorable, at the least. I drove along the coastal road for a bit before taking the route that cut over to Bayside.

When I arrived home, I sat on the patio for a while and realized I was doing everything I could to avoid going to bed, alone. Who was I kidding? I was forced to finally admit to myself that I was a lonely forty-year-old man. The truth stung as I peered up at the moon. I said, "Send me someone, okay?"

Now I was talking to the moon for God's sake!

A cloud passed in front of the moon, momentarily removing it from sight. But then the dark shadows filtered into light and once again the moonbeams appeared. I wondered if that was some kind of a sign, and if so, hopefully a good one.

At about eleven-thirty, my eyes started to get heavy. I gave in and forced myself into bed. Thankfully, I fell asleep fast. That night I had a dream about a woman in a flowing white gown. She called my name as she ran around in the rain. I raced after her but she didn't know I was trying to help so she kept running away.

Finally, she stopped running and stood still. I walked up behind her and put my hands on her shoulders. I turned her around to face me. Her head was bowed and she was crying. I forced her to look at me before gently pushing her hair away from her face. I realized the woman was Elizabeth. I wiped the tears from her cheeks and put my hand on her chin, tilting her head so I could kiss her. She needed to be kissed—and held, and protected.

After I ended the kiss, she asked softly, "Are you the one sent to save me?" She looked deep into my eyes, searching.

"Yes," I replied. I put my hand on her back and brought her close to me, and had just touched my lips to hers again before the dream ended.

Startled from being in a sound sleep, I woke up to my alarm clock radio at seven the next morning, which was set to the all news channel. I lay in bed listening to the news and the weather report and thought about the dream. It had seemed so real. Finally, I dragged myself out of bed about a half-hour later and took a long hot shower. I started to feel almost human. I brewed a cup of strong coffee and drank it, which helped to give me a kick-start.

It had always been important to me to make a good first impression, so I took my time getting dressed. I even used cologne and made sure my socks matched. Satisfied with my appearance, I grabbed a breakfast bar in the kitchen and was on my way out the door when my cell phone rang. It was McClintock. "Yes John, I'm on my way out the door now. And yes, I'll get there in plenty of time if you stop calling me!"

I had driven this route to San Francisco many times before. Lost in thought, I barely noticed the scenery as I drove. Before I knew it I was pulling up to the San

Francisco International Airport. Checking the time I realized I had almost forty-five minutes to spare before Elizabeth would arrive. I went to the Airport café, had a cup of coffee and read the paper, which turned out to be quite interesting. There was an article on the second page of the paper about Katherine O'Hara, Elizabeth to me, the interior designer from New York. The article said her husband was missing. There was a picture of the two of them together smiling. Yes, her hair was different, but those eyes, so expressive. She had high cheekbones and was extremely attractive. I was intrigued, and I had to admit, a little nervous about meeting her.

Finishing my coffee, I checked the time again. I walked to the terminal and stopped to check the arrival screens. Her flight was on time, which meant she should arrive in about five minutes. Standing at the entrance to the baggage claim area, I waited until I saw the first passengers shuffle out of the gate. As I approached I scanned the faces and spotted her. She looked anxious as she searched the sea of faces, looking for the one who recognized hers.

Elizabeth was even more beautiful than her picture and something about her made me feel like a schoolboy, something that had not happened to me for a very long time. "What was the password?" I asked myself. Finally I remembered what McClintock told me. Feeling foolish, I slowly walked toward her. She looked up as I approached. Almost next to her, I purposely dropped my pen on the floor near her and bent down to pick it up.

I said, "unicorn," and she looked right at me and asked my name. Her voice was low and sweet and she smiled at me. Our eyes met and I felt an instant connection with her. The moment seemed to be suspended in time. I felt oddly positive and happy and I hoped this particular assignment would last a long time.

I scanned the crowd of people in the terminal, looking for anything suspicious and then asked her if anyone unusual had approached her or talked to her on the plane.

"No, not really. There was this guy sitting across from me, when I woke up he was staring at me. He leered at me when I made eye contact. But I think he was harmless."

In my opinion, he was probably a disgusting pervert but I didn't want to upset her. "Just let me know if you see him again. I have to call McClintock and let him know you arrived safe and sound. He's a bit like an over-anxious father, but he's a good guy."

I called McClintock, who was relieved Elizabeth had arrived safely and reminded me—again—to be careful.

Trying to be courteous and wanting to make a good first impression, I picked up her carry-on bag and held it for her as we made friendly chatter while we walked to the car. I told her about her new house at Eureka Point and the historical places of interest in the old seaside town. She said she loved Victorian architecture. We talked as I drove and the conversation flowed easily, making it seem like we've been friends for years.

Elizabeth was cute with a teasing sense of humor. The ease of conversation made the time pass quickly and before I knew it, we were near The Inn at Cliffport. We decided we were both hungry and needed a break, so we stopped for some lunch. I visually scanned the area before we got out of the car. It was very quiet and I didn't see anyone else with the exception of an older couple coming out of the restaurant.

Dining in my favorite restaurant with her was so enjoyable that I almost forgot I was working. But I would have to keep my head about me because this was a serious assignment or else John would not have sent her to me. Knowing who she was and the circumstances that brought Elizabeth here reminded me that her safety had to be my first priority. Hopefully, the situation would work out well for her, and then perhaps we could pursue a relationship. But I was probably getting way ahead of myself. I had to mentally remind myself that I was doing my job. This was not going to be an easy assignment but it would probably be the best one I would ever have.

## Chapter Three

KATIE: FBI HEADQUARTERS, NYC

Special agent McClintock looked at me in a most serious, but caring, way from across the table as he pushed the folder over to me. He kept one finger on top of it and said, "This is your new life. Its success depends on you."

He lifted his finger off and instructed me to review the contents of the folder while he went to get a cup of coffee. I couldn't imagine what possible solution the FBI had come up with. What plan could save me from the dangerous claws of an unscrupulous drug cartel, and hopefully keep me from being linked to the crimes my husband had committed?

I sat there, my heart pounding and the blood echoing in my ears, as McClintock quietly left the room. Well, there was only one way to find out the FBI's solution. I gingerly opened the folder, as if a hasty move might alter its contents. At first my mind couldn't comprehend what I was reading. Did McClintock give me the wrong folder? I highly doubted that. He was too good to make a simple mistake like that. As I continued to read, my heart felt as if it would beat out of my chest as I realized that their plan involved me having my identity changed. *Oh my God!* In that instant everything changed, quite literally, my life would never be the same.

I had always been comfortable as Katherine O'Hara, in every aspect. My family and friends called me Katie. I had been raised Catholic and was the youngest child of an upstanding Irish family from Philadelphia. My family was large, three brothers and a sister. My parents were the epitome of what love, marriage, and success were all about. I had a deep love and respect for my family and was proud of where I came from and who I had become. Now I would become someone else.

My name would be Elizabeth Harrison, a thirty-four year-old widow whose husband died of pancreatic cancer several years ago, and whose parents had been killed in a car accident while traveling through Europe in 1979. I would have no brothers or sisters, grandparents, aunts or uncles, nieces or nephews. I was to be the sole survivor of my fictitious family. The FBI was sending me to live in a small town in Northern California named Eureka Point, a quaint and quiet seaside town that sounded lovely, but I did not imagine it as the kind of place where I could successfully start a new career and live happily. True, there had been times when I'd yearned for some peace and quiet, but never to this extreme. *Be careful what you wish for*, I thought to myself.

McClintock inched opened the door and quietly entered the room, holding a cup of coffee in his hand. His sorrowful expression sliced through me. I returned the stare as he slowly took his seat.

"It's the only way, you know." He looked me straight in the eye, forcing me to find the strength within myself to accept this. "Your husband is a very powerful man with strong underworld connections. It's safe to assume he believes you know all about his operation. It's likely he's in Costa Rica, protected by the drug lords. He has probably settled in very comfortably and has left you here to face the wolves, believing we would love nothing better than to devour you and spit you out like bad meat. When the cartel realizes that you have probably turned against your husband, and them, they will come after you. No matter where you would go they'd find you. So you have to become someone else, assume a new identity.

"You will be well taken care of Katie. Luckily, you're financially able to live in a manner that you are accustomed to. One of our best agents has been assigned to assist and protect you and a house is ready for you. The rest will be up to you. But you must never contact your family or friends, as it could put you and them in jeopardy. Do you understand this is the only way?"

"Yes, of course I understand. I'm just overwhelmed." Katie took a deep, fortifying breath as she struggled to accept this sudden and drastic turn in her life. "I can't imagine never talking to my family again. How will they even know what's happened to me?"

"I'll personally contact your parents, and without giving them the details, explain why they have not heard from you and promise them that our priority is to keep you safe. I know your parents well and I believe they have enough faith in me to trust me with your life. It would not be safe for them, or for you, to see them even once more before you go. We have to act quickly and carefully." McClintock reached across the table and laid his rough hand over mine. "I am very sorry Katie."

McClintock stood, took the folder and walked across the room to shred its contents in the machine on the desk near the door.

"Don't worry. The info is all in my computer." He smiled, pointing to his head.

I could not help myself, despite the anguish I was feeling over not being able to see my parents, I broke into a smile. McClintock was a nice man and I knew his priority was my safety. I would have to trust his judgment and instincts and do this his way. My life depended on it.

"Okay, when do I have to leave?" I asked, steeling myself for the unknown future.

McClintock explained that they were going to change my appearance right away and that I'd be on a flight to California later that evening.

"But I need to get some things together, clothes and some personal items," I protested.

McClintock shook his head. "My dear, there is no time for that. My assistant Jenny has taken care of packing a bag with some necessities for you. Whatever else you need, you can purchase after you have gotten to your new home."

I was suddenly overcome with fear and apprehension and the anxiety I felt overwhelmed me. I started to cry.

McClintock put his hand on my shoulder. "Don't worry, Katie, it will be okay. I believe all this will work out in the end I truly believe truth and justice will prevail. But it may take some time. Time for us to find Craig and bring down the cartel. Right now we must get moving on this and go have some changes made to your lovely appearance. Don't worry we're only going to make some temporary changes, like your hair and eyes. It will be relatively painless."

My head spun as we walked silently out the room and down the hall to the elevators. We entered the elevator and I watched the doors slide shut as if I was watching the curtain in a theater close at the end of the first act. We rode down the seven floors in continued silence. Honestly, what else needed to be said? I was about to become a stranger to myself and I was scared. My husband was involved in a drug cartel and had abandoned me. His actions were forcing me to leave everything I knew behind in order to survive a situation I wanted no part of. Silence, right then, was exactly what I needed as I sorted it all out in my mind.

The doors opened to a very busy area consisting of several departments including a salon. A friendly attendant greeted us at the door of the salon and ushered me to a seat. McClintock remarked I'd make a terrific blond and chuckled. Stella, the stylist, thought I'd be better off with inconspicuous brown hair. We compromised and settled on a warm golden blonde shade.

"Now, what about the cut?" Stella asked, trying to sound positive.

I had very long auburn hair that people always complimented me on. My hair had always been my signature feature. I endured the change better then I'd expected as Stella dyed, cut and styled my hair. Thankfully, she did a good job and did not cut too much off the length. The layered style floated around my face in a way I actually liked.

I thanked her before McClintock took me to the eye lab where Dr. Greenberg replaced my designer eyeglasses with colored contacts. A lifetime of green eyes were now blue and when I took in my reflection I saw someone neatly unrecognizable staring back at me.

A few more changes and Katie was completely gone, replaced by this new person. Elizabeth.

McClintock nodded with approval and told me I looked like the perfect California girl. "You'll fit right in there. I just hope you're not too gorgeous. We don't want you drawing too much attention to yourself."

Jenny, McClintock's assistant, walked into the finishing room with my travel bag, a new purse, and a change of clothing. McClintock had me go through the contents of my purse, in which was a wallet containing a temporary California driver's license in the name of Katherine Harrison, a new Social Security card, several credit cards, a bank card, and a health insurance card. He handed me a key case and told me it contained my house and car keys.

"What kind of car does she, uh, do I drive?" I asked in a wry tone.

"It's a VW so don't get too excited," McClintock replied.

I stepped into the dressing room and put on my change of clothing, which included jeans, a longed-sleeved button tee, a lightweight jacket, and a pair of stylish running shoes. McClintock was waiting for me when I came out. He said he liked my new look and snapped a picture with his camera phone.

In a serious tone McClintock told me the name of my contact in San Francisco, a guy by the name of Tom Owens, who would identify himself with the password, "unicorn". Tom and I would meet at the airport arrival gate and he would then drive me to Eureka Point.

My flight was set to leave La Guardia in less than an hour and a half. We rushed down to the parking garage, jumped in a dark sedan and McClintock drove me to the airport. As I gazed out the window, the wipers rhythmically slapped the rain off the windshield. I already missed my mom and dad. Emotionally, I was still reeling from the shock of what my "beloved" husband had done and now I could not even go to my mom for comforting support, which she had always given me, especially in times of trouble. Feeling alone and very sad, unable to hold back my emotional distress, tears welled up in my eyes and then rolled down my cheeks.

"You're thinking about your parents aren't you?" McClintock asked, breaking the silence. "The best I can offer you is the promise I will explain to them that what we have done was out of necessity and in your best interest. They know you love them. Hopefully some day you will be able to see them again. It will be really hard, but it's the only way."

"I appreciate what you've done for me. I really do. And I won't forget your kindness, ever. Thank you."

McClintock smiled at me and said, "You're welcome. You know, usually I've helped complete strangers do this. But this time it's personal. You can thank me by keeping strong, being careful, and by making your new life a good one. Tom, your contact in San Francisco, is a good friend of mine. He's also the best agent we have doing this kind of thing. I'd trust him with my life so I feel pretty good about trusting him with yours."

The car slowed and I realized we were at the airport already. After parking the car in a special "official use" garage behind the gate, we entered the boarding area. McClintock showed the boarding attendant his ID and handed her my ticket. He gave me wink and a smile and just like that, he was gone. I was alone—completely alone and terrified.

The attendant helped me board and escorted me to my seat, thankfully in first class. Maybe I could finally get some sleep. I had not slept in over twenty hours and was totally exhausted and strung out emotionally.

The other passengers were boarding the plane and soon everyone was seated and beverages were served. Never had a diet Coke and a bag of pretzels tasted so good. Captain Johnson came on the loud speaker and welcomed the passengers on the flight from New York to San Francisco and told us we would be taking off in a few short minutes. As the plane's engines revved in preparation for takeoff, I took one last look out at the New York City skyline and hoped for better things to come my way. McClintock had said it correctly. This would be my new life and it was up to me whether or not it would be a success. As a survival tactic I decided I would take McClintock's advice to think positively and be strong. That was the only way I would be able to survive this life-changing ordeal.

Thankfully the flight was quiet and uneventful. After a light supper, I fell asleep, ironically missing most of the in-flight movie about a fugitive wrongfully accused of his wife's murder. I felt like an innocent fugitive on the run, and I got angry at the thought of being put in this position knowing it was Craig's doing. I decided I would not allow myself to give up on my life, just to spite my husband. If I chose to be angry and miserable about it, then I would be successful in allowing Craig to take everything I held dear away from me. I'd given up so much already. I found some solace in the thought he would someday be found and brought to justice.

Nevertheless, it was difficult to think about all the love and support I had given Craig over the last few years to now realize he most likely had never returned that love and had probably just used me. But I would get over it. I had to. What doesn't kill you makes you stronger, right?

The Captain came over the loud speaker again and informed us we would be landing at the San Francisco International Airport in approximately ten minutes. As the seven-forty-seven gently made its descent, I searched my purse for a comb, having some difficulty getting used to a new purse and where things were in it. Previously, I had a favorite purse I had used for the last five years.

I combed my hair and touched up my make-up, and, as I peered into my compact mirror, I was taken back, momentarily forgetting my new appearance. I hoped I would grow accustomed to my new look. It's disconcerting to have looked at myself for thirty-four years and then suddenly not recognize my own eyes or hair.

I caught the man sitting across the aisle leering at me as I re-applied my lipstick. I threw a quick, disapproving look his way and he smirked at me. Men can be so superficial, I thought to myself. Must be the blond hair.

My thoughts turned to the future. Soon I would be meeting my contact, Tom Owens. I wondered what he would be like. He would know who I was because McClintock had taken my picture in the hallway and transmitted it to Tom's cell phone. He would identify himself to me with the password 'unicorn.' I laughed to myself finding amusement in being given a password like a spy. I had always enjoyed reading a good espionage and suspense story. Now I was living one.

The plane made a perfect landing and the Captain thanked us for traveling with him and his crew. As soon as the plane came to a stop, I retrieved my travel bag and made my way to the exit. Walking through the terminal and into the baggage claim area, I felt a bit anxious, like the slight nervousness I would feel before meeting with a new client. I searched the crowd and finally saw a tall, attractive man with dark blond hair who was headed in my direction. I hoped he was my contact, Tom Owens. As the man got close to me he slowed his pace, stopped near me, and dropped a pen on the floor. As he bent down to pick it up, he peered up at me and quietly said "unicorn."

Relieved he was my contact I replied, "Does the unicorn have a name?"

The man smiled and said, "Hi, I'm Tom Owens, a friend of John McClintock's. You must be Elizabeth. Do you prefer Elizabeth or Liz?" I had to really think about that question, and the answer. Nervously grinning, I said I wasn't sure yet. He smiled and laughed.

"Welcome to California!" Tom exclaimed, immediately breaking the ice and making me feel at ease. Except in Craig's case, I had always been a good judge of character. Tom seemed like a decent, friendly guy, and was hopefully someone I could count on as I plunged into my new life. Or at least I hoped that would be so.

# Chapter Four

ELIZABETH, SAN FRANCISCO, CALIFORNIA

Tom told me he thought I would really like Eureka Point and my new house, describing it as "awesome." "The house is up on a hill and the views down to the water are fantastic. You have a view of the point of the peninsula from your back terrace. The house was just completed a few months ago. You're the first owner. I don't want to give everything away, so I won't say any more about the house. Let's just go so you can see it firsthand."

Tom picked up my carry-on bag and we walked outside to the parking lot. His car, an official use black Buick, was parked in a special spot right outside the front of the airport. Like a perfect gentleman, he opened the passenger door for me to get in and put my bag on the back seat. I felt safe and secure and mentally thanked McClintock for using Tom as my contact. It was almost as if I had met him before. He seemed familiar somehow. He was rather good looking, not drop dead handsome, but tall and well built with very intense blue eyes. He looked right at me when he spoke and came across as being direct and honest. Successfully living alone in a new place was going to be a real challenge. Having a good friend would be nice. I hoped he would become one.

We drove out of the San Francisco area and up the coastal highway. All the while, Tom pointed out places of interest. "Eureka Point is about fifty miles North of San Francisco. The drive will take about an hour and a half, but the scenery is fantastic the entire way and you'll get a chance to see some great sights. We'll stop along the way for some lunch." I asked Tom where he lived. He told me he lived in a town not too far North of Eureka called Bayside. "This whole area of Northern California is really the most beautiful countryside I have ever seen, and I've traveled a lot. The pace is slower. The people are much more laid back than they are on the East Coast. It takes some getting used to, but I think you'll really like it here."

"Yes, I agree, from what I've seen so far." Embarrassed, I realized I was staring at Tom. "I must admit, I pictured you as older, and very serious. McClintock thinks you're the best at this."

"Oh really? Well, I'll try to live up to his expectations, and yours."

I inquired about how long he had known McClintock.

"Oh, we go way back. I'm originally from Framingham, Massachusetts, about thirty miles outside of Boston. John's from Boston. We met at the police academy and both ended up becoming involved in undercover work and the FBI. He was the best man in my wedding."

I felt a bit of a let down thinking that Tom was married. I didn't suffer my disappointment long. With a forlorn look on his face and a deep sadness in his eyes, Tom added, "My wife had terminal lung cancer and passed away almost three years ago. After that, I decided to relocate to the West Coast to be near my sister and her family. John and his wife, Elise, helped me get through the ordeal of my wife's illness and death."

"I'm sorry. That must have been so difficult for you to have to go through."

"It was. But I had a lot of support, like I said. And now things are pretty good." He managed a smile, while his eyes stayed on me for an extended moment. Tom had been right in saying that the drive would be enjoyable. It was a clear, beautiful day and the sky was a magnificent shade of blue. The Pacific Ocean was on one side, and steep hills and cliffs on the other side which made for a dramatic and breathtaking scene. Temperatures were in the mid-seventies with no humidity. Tom turned the radio on and I felt oddly relaxed, considering the circumstances that had brought me to this place.

My mind wandered and a strange feeling came over me, almost as if I was dreaming. Tom asked me what I was thinking about. "Oh, I feel a bit uneasy having been thrown into this strange situation." I was not sure exactly how much McClintock had told Tom about my circumstances. I curiously asked him what he knew about me.

"I know McClintock sent you here with a new identity for your own protection. John really cares about you. He told me you're like a daughter to him. I'm aware that your husband is missing and a wanted criminal because of his involvement with a large South American drug cartel. You can trust me Elizabeth," he added. At that point I realized I couldn't identify with the name Elizabeth, but Lizzie appealed to me. "You can call me Lizzie," I announced.

"Lizzie, it's a pleasure to meet you," Tom replied with a funny smirk on his face. We both laughed out loud. It felt good to laugh, to let myself go and actually have a jovial moment, especially after the tenseness I had been dealing with for the last few days. Tom told me he was serious about being able to trust him, that it was his job to protect me and see I had everything I needed to start a new life for myself. I thanked Tom for his kindness and told him I was glad to be able to count on someone.

We came upon a more populated area with charming inns, wineries and restaurants. We were both rather hungry so we stopped at The Inn at Cliffport for some lunch. Tom parked the car and we walked slowly across the parking lot, admiring the view of the sparkling ocean. Upon entering the Inn, I marveled at the warmth and charm of the place. Tom requested a table by the window. A friendly young woman waited on us and Tom took the liberty of ordering us each a glass of wine.

"It's from a local winery and a specialty of the Inn. I really like this place, the food, this wine, and the atmosphere. I especially enjoy coming here for dinner and watch the lighthouse beacon as it shines on the water, it's very relaxing.

"Maybe you'd like to come here with me for dinner some night, after you get situated."

"That would be great. It's a beautiful Inn. I can understand why you enjoy coming here. How close are we to Eureka Point?"

"It's about a fifteen minute drive from here."

The glasses of wine arrived and Tom made a toast to my new life. We clanged our glasses together and I sipped some of the flavorful wine. "This is very good."

"I'm glad you approve."

Tom told me stories about the area, of shipwrecks and the ghosts of old sea captains, and of course, lost treasures reported to be in the area. Looking out at the view of the cliffs and Pacific Ocean, it wasn't hard to believe such tales.

Our food arrived and we both ate every bite of our deliciously prepared seafood. We finished our meals and I decided to stop in the ladies room before we left the Inn. When I returned to the table Tom had already paid the bill and handed me a package. I looked in the bag and was delighted to see that he had purchased a bottle of the wine we had enjoyed so much with our lunch. "It's a housewarming gift for you," Tom said. I appreciated his thoughtfulness and told him so.

We walked to the car and were soon on our way again, back on the coastal highway. We drove for a few minutes when a storm rolled in from the ocean, turning the sky a dark and ominous shade, like cold blue steel. The breeze turned into a blustery cold wind and the temperature dropped dramatically. We closed the windows as big splats of rain hit the windshield. Tom switched on the wipers as the rain turned into a downpour. A shiver ran down my spine. Tom slowed down and drove carefully as the highway curved first one way and then the other. I noticed a truck coming down the other side of the highway with its headlights on and I could hear its horn blowing continuously. I realized the truck was speeding out of control and heading in our direction. Tom tried to pull over but there was not enough room on our side of the highway. Terrified, I screamed. Tom quickly responded and steered across the highway to where there was more room. He managed to get us out of the way of the truck, but we swerved and slammed sideways into a tree. That was the last thing I remembered.

When I regained consciousness I slowly opened my dazed eyes and focused on Tom. I was horrified when I saw a he was bleeding from a large gash on his forehead.

His airbag had inflated, which he was slumped into, and he was unconscious. I grabbed his cell phone and punched in nine-one-one. I was unsure of our exact location I tried to give our location to the operator, but I only knew that we were headed up the Pacific Coast Highway and were about ten minutes North of Cliffside. Luckily, the emergency operator explained she had a fix on our location because Tom's cell phone had a GPS tracking system. I put the cell phone down to take care of the gash on Tom's forehead. I knew I had to apply pressure to the open wound to stop the bleeding.

Grabbing my case from the backseat, I quickly unzipped it and pulled out a t-shirt. When I applied pressure to the bleeding gash, Tom winced but didn't regain consciousness. Panic-stricken, I had to force myself to calm down. I took a few deep breaths and regained my composure. As I picked up the cell phone with my other hand, I noticed I had been cut. The bottle of wine I had been holding must have smashed during the accident. I grabbed a sock from my case and wrapped it around my hand as best as I could. I checked on Tom again. The bleeding had stopped but his breathing was shallow and he still didn't open his eyes. When I finally picked the cell phone up again, the operator informed me an ambulance would be there momentarily. She asked me my name and I stuttered, finally able to mutter Elizabeth.

I could see two sets of flashing ambulance lights in the distance and realized the driver of the truck might have hit something or swerved off the road also. One of the ambulances finally reached our car and two medics sprang into action. I yelled that I was not badly hurt but explained that Tom was still unconscious and had lost quite a bit of blood. They pried his door open and amazingly had him on a stretcher and in the ambulance in less than two minutes.

One of the medics helped me into the ambulance and took a look at my hand. She determined a few stitches at the hospital would take care of my injury. I asked about Tom's condition and was told by the other medic that his blood pressure was normal but his pupils were not reacting to light. The medic explained it was probably due to a concussion. They put Tom on an intravenous saline solution and monitored his heart rate and blood pressure.

We finally arrived at the Eureka Hospital Emergency Room and they quickly wheeled Tom into a trauma room. A nurse cleaned up my hand and a resident stitched it up. The nurse wrapped my hand in gauze. She smiled at me kindly, put the remaining gauze roll in a plastic bag and told me I should take it home with me. I went to the front desk to give them my insurance information and was then released. I again inquired about Tom's condition and was told he was stable but unresponsive at the present time. This concerned me. I wanted to stay in case Tom regained consciousness, but I was told I should go home and could call later to get an update on his condition.

I picked up all my belongings, which consisted of my purse, carry-on bag, and the plastic bag with the gauze inside, and went to the waiting room to sit down and mull over my situation. Deciding I would have to call a cab, I asked an orderly where I could find a phone. He directed me to a public phone area. I looked up taxi companies in the Yellow Pages and called the first number listed. The driver showed up outside the hospital entrance in less than five minutes. I got into the cab and gave the driver my address, "Eighteen-hundred Hillside Drive, Eureka Point."

The driver was overly friendly and talkative, something I would normally have found comforting, but my mind was racing and I couldn't concentrate on his mindless chatter. We finally came to a pair of stone constructed walls on each side of the road with an opening to a very large area of properties with new homes. The sign read "Eureka Point, Premier Homes by La Hacienda Builders." The taxi driver pulled onto Hillside Drive and up to the top of the hill. The houses, mostly European in design, were separated from each other by trees, shrubs, and plants which allowed for privacy. Each house was unique in its layout and design and they all appeared to be very elegant.

Finally we came to eighteen hundred Hillside Drive and my new home. It was a French country style house and I thought it looked awesome, just as Tom had described it. The driver pulled into the driveway and parked in front of the stone walkway that led to the front door. I paid him the fare plus a nice tip. I grabbed my things and pulled the keys out of my purse. The taxi pulled away and I stood there facing my house, admiring it. The neighborhood and surrounding area was beautiful, very serene and picturesque.

      I slowly walked up the front walk and to the front door. It was almost dark but the outside lights had been turned on, as was a light on inside the house. I slipped the key into the lock and turned the brass handle until it clicked in my hand and the door opened. The house was gorgeous. The foyer was painted in a warm rustic gold tone with ivy leaves and grapevines stenciled on the walls. There was a semi-circular staircase on one side and French doors that led to a sunroom on the other. A note was on a desk under the stair wall. It was from Tom, welcoming me. Almost as if he knew he might not be able to be here with me when I first arrived here, he wrote instructions for me to look in the zippered pocket on the inside of my purse to find the code for the alarm system. Tom had thought of every detail and covered all the bases. I found the code in my purse and walked down the hall to the kitchen. Luckily we had a similar security system in our house in New York. It took me only a few minutes to figure out how to use this one. I went back to the entrance and turned the alarm on first making sure the front door was locked. Then I took a tour of my new home.

The living room was the first room down the hallway from the foyer. The rustic French theme had been continued in there. The furniture in the living room was elegant, so much so that it clashed with the rustic color and texture of the room. I would have to make some changes to the living room as soon as possible. Being an interior designer, I was a perfectionist that way.

On the other side of the hallway, across from the living room, was a gorgeous dining room that was wallpapered in a stunning burgundy damask material. The drapes were a deep raspberry silk and the sheers looked to be imported European lace. I walked back to the foyer and up the dramatic spiral staircase. At the top of the stairs and to the right was the master bedroom that was decorated in a very feminine style. The furniture was French Provincial and absolutely gorgeous. The windows had wooden shutters at the bottoms and lace sheers at the rounded tops. I wasn't too thrilled with the shutters, but I guessed I could live with them for a while. At least I would have privacy in my bedroom and not have to worry about nosey neighbors watching me.

Across the hall from the master bedroom was a very large bathroom with a reproduction European claw foot tub, a walk-in shower and a lot of Italian marble. On the outside wall of the bathroom there was an oval window that was designed in stained glass that swirled around in deep shades of indigo blue, brilliant green and purple, reminding me of a peacock tail feather. An antique looking walnut vanity housed an ornately decorated marble oval sink. The bathroom was the most beautiful I had ever seen. I couldn't wait to take a nice warm soak in the luxurious tub.

A little further down the hall from the bathroom was a second bedroom I would probably use as a guestroom or studio. Across from that was a walk-in linen closet filled with sheets, blankets, and bath towels. It appeared I also had everything I would need in the way of shampoo, soap and other toiletries as well. The closet was fully stocked.

Realizing I was totally exhausted, I walked back to the master bedroom and sat down on the bed. Using the phone on the night table next to my bed, I called the hospital and inquired Tom's status and was told he was still listed in serious condition. There had been no change from when he had been admitted. At least he was not critical or worse. *Poor man*, I thought, *and so nice too*. I was already missing his company.

The European claw foot tub in the master bathroom had looked so inviting and luxurious that I decided to relax in a hot bath for a few minutes before going to bed. After taking a nice hot soak, I dried off and checked the dresser drawers to see what was in them. To my surprise, there were a few pairs of panties in my size, some pajamas, a robe and sport clothes. I grabbed the pajamas, put them on and then opened the doors to the closet. Inside were several outfits in my size and three pairs of shoes. McClintock had certainly done a great job of making sure I would have everything I needed.

I went through my bag quickly and discovered that Tom's cell phone was in there. I made sure it was turned on and put it on the night table next to the bed. I took the contacts out of my eyes and put them into their case. Then, slipping into bed, totally exhausted, I was out like a light.

# Chapter Five

LIZZIE, EUREKA POINT, CALIFORNIA

    I was startled out of a deep sleep by the sound of an unfamiliar ring tone. Groggy, I sat up and tried to get my bearings. When I saw the French Provincial furniture and beautiful surroundings, I remembered where I was. The display screen on Tom's cell phone indicated it was McClintock. I pushed the button to accept the call, but just to be on the safe side, I didn't say anything at first. After a few seconds I recognized McClintock's voice.

    "Are you there Tom?"

    "This is Elizabeth Harrison. Tom and I were in a car accident yesterday on our way to Eureka Point. He was driving and swerved out of the way of an out of control truck and we hit a tree.

    "He's in the hospital suffering from a concussion and was still unconscious last night. I'm going to call the hospital and check on his condition this morning."

    "Are you okay Elizabeth?" McClintock asked with concern.

    "Yes, I only had a minor cut on my hand they stitched up in the ER. I took a cab home last night. Other than what happened to poor Tom, everything is okay. I'm no worse for the wear."

McClintock gave me information about my cell phone, bank account, and other legal matters that Tom would have advised me about if he were able to. He also told me I should only answer my cell phone when the call was from a number I had programmed in and if I knew who the caller was.

"If you see anyone suspicious or feel that something is not right, contact me right away. Please call me after you've checked on Tom. Be careful and I'll talk to you later."

"I will. Goodbye." I got out of bed and took a steamy shower, dried, dressed, put in my contacts and changed the dressing on my hand. I put on a lavender jogging set, my new running shoes and then called the hospital to inquire about Tom's condition. I was told he had regained consciousness and the neurologist was scheduled to examine him shortly. He had been upgraded from serious to stable condition. I sighed in relief and asked the nurse if Tom could have a visitor. She told me he could and explained what the visiting hours were. I looked at the clock and realized I could still see him that morning if I left soon.

I grabbed my purse and found the car keys. I went down the spiral staircase marveling again at the décor. I stopped in the kitchen and found my new cell phone, charged and ready to go, just where McClintock had told me it would be, and then proceeded to the garage after resetting the security system. My new car was a maroon VW Passat. As I got in the car I noticed there was an automatic garage door opener control on the dashboard, which was a convenience that helped me feel secure. As I pulled out of the driveway I felt strong and content in the knowledge that Tom, having regained consciousness, would probably be released from the hospital soon and then I could really relax and feel comfortable enough to enjoy my new home and my new life.

I remembered how the cab had brought me from the hospital the night before, and with the help of the blue hospital signs, I had no problem finding my way. Seeing the sights around the charming old town of Eureka on a sunny and bright morning added to my good mood. I passed the elementary school and saw young children happily playing outside for recess. Around the corner was a lovely little church. The pastor was outside admiring his garden and he waived at me as I passed by. As I smiled and returned a waive I thought to myself, "I'm going to like this place." The town was quaint and welcoming. The Victorian houses were painted in deep stunning colors that you couldn't help but notice and the entire town had a nostalgic and romantic feel to it. Flags flapped in the breeze, birds were singing happily, and people were out jogging or riding bikes. The air was fresh and clean, smelling of flowers and cut grass with just a hint of the scent of the ocean nearby. Right at that moment everything felt right with the world.

I arrived at the hospital and pulled into the parking lot, stopping to get a ticket from the parking attendant. She asked me if I was visiting a patient and gave me directions to the area where Tom's room was located. I walked into the hospital and took the elevator to the second floor and followed the signs to the area where Tom's room was located. A young nurse smiled and asked if I needed assistance. She gave me Tom's room number and explained the neurologist was just completing his exam. She then showed me to a small waiting area across from Tom's room. In less than a minute, the door to Tom's room opened and the doctor came out. I stood up and approached him. The doctor introduced himself as Dr. Howard Brown, Head of Neurology, and asked me to sit back down with him in the waiting area so he could explain about Tom's condition and prognosis.

Dr. Brown told me Tom's vital signs were very good and that Tom claimed he felt fine, except for a headache, which often accompanies a concussion. The doctor then told me a CT scan had revealed some bleeding around Tom's brain, but nothing he considered unusually alarming. The worst symptoms would probably subside in a few days. "Mr. Owens seems a bit out of it yet, but I am hopeful. We're going to keep him for a few days for observation." Dr. Brown then told me I could go in to see Tom. I thanked him and entered the room.

Tom had been gazing out of the window, but when the door opened he turned and smiled at me. I quickly went over and sat beside the bed and asked him how he was feeling.

"I feel pretty good, a bit of a headache. The neurologist told me I have a concussion. I don't remember the accident. Are you an intern?"

Thinking Tom was joking I said, "Right, that will be part of my new M. O., Dr. Harrison."

"I must really be out of it doc, 'cause I don't get the joke." My heart sank. Tom did not know who I was. I felt the blood draining from my head and was nauseous and lightheaded. I tried to compose myself as to not alarm him and said, "Well Mr. Owens, I'll let you get some rest." Tom asked me if I could stay and keep him company. Promising him I would stop in to see him again, I forced a smile and left the room. Dr. Brown was at the nurse's station and I quickly went over and told him that Tom had not known who I was.

Quite matter-of-factly Dr. Brown replied, "Post-traumatic amnesia can accompany the type of blow to the head Mr. Owens' suffered. He will hopefully start to remember things as time passes." On that note, Dr. Brown smiled and excused himself, telling me he had other patients to check on.

Sitting in the waiting area, I could see Tom through the long window panel in the door to his room. I knew I had been developing a friendship with him in the short time we had known each other. I had felt an instant connection with him the moment we had met. Now I would have to accept the fact that I had only myself to depend on for a while. Things were not going to be as easy as they looked like they were going to be just fifteen minutes earlier. *How quickly things can change.* I was having that lesson stuffed down my throat a lot recently. I could break down and cry, or carry on. I didn't really have a choice.

I left the hospital feeling dismayed, as if I had lost my best friend, again. When I got into the car I called McClintock but received his voicemail. I felt it would be best not to leave a message. I was probably being paranoid, but better to be safe than sorry. I would have to try to reach McClintock later.

I stopped at a supermarket and bought some food, clothes detergent and a few other necessities. I saw the *National Tribune* with the headline, "New York Entrepreneur Craig Montgomery Flees Country." I picked up the paper and read how Craig was on the FBI's most wanted list. The article said he had been linked to a South American drug smuggling cartel and had fled the country after federal drug enforcement officials had learned of his involvement in the laundering of millions of dollars and the killing of at least two FBI agents. It went on to say I was missing and speculate that I might have been killed because of my knowledge of the operations of the drug cartel. Another article, an opinion piece, promoted the suspicion that I could have been in on the operation and ran off to South America with my husband. It made me sick to think people who actually knew me, friends and relatives, might believe that of me. And there was our picture; the two of us at a friend's wedding, smiling and looking like the perfect successful couple. That was in happier times, long before I knew. I felt like a fool.

I decided a shopping trip might take my mind off things for a while. The young checkout girl told me there were some good shops in town on the main street. I asked her how to get there and she kindly gave me directions. I thanked her and was on my way. I needed a diversion.

# Chapter Six

EUREKA POINT, CALIFORNIA

Eureka Point was surrounded on three sides by water. The actual town of Eureka was near the center of the peninsula and my house was closer to the end. It was a beautiful and scenic area, quite quaint but with a definite air of sophistication. Driving into town and admiring the sights, I realized this area of Northern California was probably somewhere I would have handpicked myself, to live, build a house, and raise a family. Craig had been the socialite, preferring the hustle and bustle of the east and New York City. Then of course, "business" was probably much better in the busiest city in the country.

No wonder we had lived so extravagantly. I used to wonder how we could live in the manner in which we had, but then I would rationalize that Craig was a good businessman and his restaurants and wise investments were paying off. Now I realized I had been naïve and felt foolish for not paying more attention to what had been going on. Those strange feelings I had felt over the years had been warnings. I was an intuitive woman but had just not realized it. I vowed to pay more attention to everything for now on and to trust my instincts.

As I approached the main part of town I saw several interesting shops and restaurants, so I parked the VW, got out and started walking. I came upon an interior design shop. Very intrigued, I decided to go in and check it out. As I opened the door to go inside, a door chime announced my arrival.

A handsome young man with blond California hair and piercing blue eyes looked up and smiled, asking if he could assist me. I smiled back and told him I was a self-taught interior designer and had just moved into the area. "Are you decorating a new home?" he asked politely.

"Well, I purchased it already decorated and I like the style, but I may want to add my own personal touches. I'm just looking around right now. " He told me to take my time and to ask if I had any questions.

A display shelf of decorating books and magazines caught my eye. I smiled as I picked up a magazine that pictured one of the rooms I had decorated for Carly on Long Island which read, "Katie O'Hara's take on cottage by the sea." The young man who had greeted me looked up and noticed what I was looking at and said, "Oh, my boss is always talking about that designer, Katie O'Hara. Did you read she was either kidnapped, missing or ran away because the Feds were looking for her husband in connection with drug smuggling? I just know she wasn't involved in anything like that. You can tell she's a nice person, can't you?" I gulped and nodded affirmatively.

I walked around the shop feeling very much at home and in my element and purchased a pair of kitchen curtains in a beautiful sage green toile. They would fit very nicely into the French country theme of my new kitchen. As I approached the counter, I saw a "Help Wanted" sign near the register. I told the young man I might be interested in applying for the position. He asked me for my name and phone number, telling me his boss was out on a job but would probably call me when she returned. I picked up the shop's business card and programmed the phone number into my cell phone, thanking the young man for his assistance.

Driving home I spotted a florist's shop and decided to stop in. I bought a bouquet of fresh flowers to put in the kitchen. The flowers would add some nice color, and besides, they smelled wonderful!

As I drove home, the winds really picked up and it became quite stormy looking. Just as I pulled into the driveway, it started to pour. Using the automatic garage door opener, I was able to pull right into the garage. I entered the house and turned off the security alarm. I locked the door and reset the alarm. My new home was safe and efficient and I felt secure. It was a good feeling.

My cell phone rang and I recognized the phone number as the one for the design shop. When I answered the phone, a woman identified herself as Carol from "Chateau Chic" and she apologized for sounding awful. She explained she had a bad cold. She asked me a few questions about my decorating knowledge and experience, which I intentionally played down, and we arranged to meet and discuss the open position at two o'clock the following afternoon at the shop.

Just as I sat down in the kitchen, my cell phone rang again. It was the phone number for the hospital and I answered it, hoping it would be Tom's doctor or a nurse giving me an update. To my surprise, it was Tom himself! "Lizzie, are you okay?"

"Yes, I'm just fine and settling down nicely in my new place, but I've been very concerned about you."

Tom told me he had fallen asleep after lunch and had slept for about three hours. When he woke, he remembered everything. He had contacted McClintock to tell him that he was okay. "Lizzie, the doctor is going to release me tomorrow morning and I was hoping you could come pick me up and drive me to my home in Bayside. The car was totaled in the accident."

"Of course I will. I'm so relieved you're okay. I was really worried." We talked for a few more minutes and arranged I would pick him up at the hospital at nine a.m., and drive him home, which was about a twenty-minute drive from Eureka. I would need to be back for my appointment with Carol at Chateau Chic by 2:00 p.m.

I was really relieved Tom was okay and had gotten his memory back. It had been a strange turn of events on top of such a traumatic experience. Sitting down in the living room with a cup of tea, I put my feet up and daydreamed of how my life would unfold. I drifted off to sleep and was startled awake by a loud crashing noise. It had still been light outside when I fell asleep, and as I had not intended to fall asleep, I had not turned any lights on. I was in the dark and had to fumble around until I found the lamp, to my dismay the light would not turn on. The electricity must have gone off. Anxious but somewhat relieved, I cringed as an intense lightning bolt lit up the sky and an ominous crash of thunder shook the floor. I realized the sound that had woken me up was thunder and not something worse.

Trying to make my way over to the long table behind the love seat where I had seen a candleholder and candle, I stumbled over the ottoman and whacked the side of my ankle right on the bone. The sudden intense pain made me yell out loud. Losing my balance, I fell on the floor. I just sat there for a few minutes trying to pull myself together. My eyes finally adjusted to the darkness and I was able to make my way over to the table behind the love seat and felt around for a pack of matches in the drawer. I was able to light the candle and carried it with me as I made my way to the kitchen. As I walked down the hall I could feel the warm moistness of blood seeping out of the gash.

I went back into the kitchen and cleaned up my ankle with a wet paper towel. Peering out the window I was amazed to see a large tree had been cut nearly in half and was smoldering in the darkness. It must have been struck by lightning. In the distance I could see clouds charging in front of the moon. It was quite windy but the thunder had stopped and I could see lightening off in the distance. Thinking the worst was over I sat down at the kitchen table, ravenous. I would wait awhile to see if the electricity would come back on so I could make something for dinner.

My cell phone rang and the number on the screen showed the hospital number again, so I answered. "Hello," nothing. "Hello," nothing. I was about to push the button to end the call when I heard a very low muffled voice say in an eerie tone, "I know who you are."

Impulsively, I was about to demand to know the identity of the caller but my instincts stopped me. Whoever it was, they might have my cell phone number but that did not mean they knew who I was, and more importantly, where I was. I waited and listened. They said nothing for a few moments and then I heard the angry muffled male voice say, "Bitch, I'm going to find you and when I do, I'll send you back home to McClintock in pieces!" and the call ended.

Slumping back in the chair in terror, my heart racing, the events of the last several days finally taking their toll, I broke down and cried.

# Chapter Seven

EUREKA POINT, CALIFORNIA

I sobbed like a baby, on the verge of hysteria, until I came to my senses, realizing I could be wasting valuable time. Grabbing my cell phone, I called the last phone number in my phone's memory, which was the hospital's main number. I reached a receptionist at the main desk and asked to speak with Mr. Owens in room one-twenty-one. The receptionist put me on hold. She came back on the line a few moments later and told me Mr. Owens had been moved to a semi-private room earlier that evening. She would connect me to his new room.

It was possible whoever had called me may have done so from the room after Tom had been taken to his new room. I believed it was possible for someone to find out the last number that had been called from a particular phone. Whoever had called me was someone who was looking for me, and they were getting way too close. I shuddered at the thought of some sleazy underworld tough guy sent by the drug cartel to find me. Or, just as bad or worse, Craig furiously was coming to get me.

I was relieved to hear Tom's voice when he answered the phone. After I finished explaining to him what had happened, he asked me some questions in rapid succession: Where was I? Was the alarm on? Who, if anyone, had I given my cell phone number to? After I answered his questions he gave me explicit instructions. He told me to turn my cell phone off and to use his instead, the one I had brought home with me from the hospital after the accident. I was to screen every call and only answer if it was Tom himself or McClintock. He would call McClintock and let him know what had happened. Tom assured me it was not possible for someone to find out my location from my cell phone number unless it had a tracking device installed, which mine did not.

Tom made me feel better, but before we ended our conversation he asked me if I had any experience using a handgun. "A gun? Heck no, I never needed to carry a gun before," I said hesitantly.

"Well, there's a first time for everything. You probably won't need to use it, but you should know how to, just in case," Tom urged.

Because I had no real experience with a gun, Tom gave me a crash course on the basics over the phone and then told me there was a loaded handgun with the safety on in the bottom drawer of the dressing table in my bedroom.

After we ended our conversation I immediately turned off my cell phone and went upstairs with the lit candle, found the gun and grabbed Tom's cell phone and brought them both back downstairs with me to the kitchen. I decided I could not wait for the electricity to come back on so I made a peanut butter and jelly sandwich. After I finished eating I decided to take up residence in the living room and I lit a fire, which would serve two purposes, light and heat. It had become chilly after the storm.

Exhausted, I lied down on the sofa and put the gun next to me on the coffee table. Because I was more tired than I was afraid, I fell fast asleep. I slept until the morning sun came streaming in the large front window. Groggy, I opened my eyes and saw the beautiful sunrise and wondered if the previous night had been a dream. As I slowly looked around I saw the gun on the coffee table and was brought back to the harsh reality of my situation. The fire in the fireplace had gone out and the candles had burnt out, now just stubs in their holders. I yawned, stretched and picked up Tom's phone and the gun and went into the kitchen to make a pot of coffee. Thankfully, the electricity had come back on and I was able to cook a decent breakfast.

As I ate breakfast, I gazed out the back window and could see that the storm had done considerable damage. Trees were down and debris was scattered everywhere. The tree that had been split in half by lightening was nothing but a black silhouette against the blue and green backdrop of the sky and meadow.

Tom's cell phone rang and I was glad to see McClintock's name appear on the screen. I accepted the call but did not say anything until McClintock said, "It's okay, it's me."

He felt I was in no immediate danger and suggested I purchase a new cell phone and get a new phone number. He had alerted the local police. They would keep an eye out for any suspicious activity near my house. Tom would be released from the hospital and lived only ten minutes and a phone call away, and he was having local FBI agents investigate as well. As usual, McClintock was on top of the situation and taking care of every detail. I thanked him for his help.

After I got off the phone I realized I had less than an hour to shower, dress and get to the hospital to pick up Tom. I took the cell phone and the gun up to the bathroom with me and took a very quick shower. As I shampooed my hair I kept thinking about that scene in "Psycho" where that poor woman is murdered while she's taking a shower, and in my mind I kept envisioning Craig attacking me. I knew the house was secure but I could not shake the feeling of uneasiness I had.

Feeling better to be out of the house, I rather enjoyed the drive to the hospital. At least I could relax for awhile. When I got to Tom's room he was all packed and ready to leave.

"In a hurry to get out of here?" I joked. Tom looked at me very strangely and for a moment had me believing he thought I was a doctor again. "I'm glad to see you're back to your old self and mischievous ways," I chided.

We left the hospital and drove to Tom's house in Bayside. His house was a small but very nicely appointed cottage outside of the little town of Bayside. I could see the bay from his house and the area was lovely and picturesque. It was not hard to understand why he loved living here. We went inside, sat down at the kitchen table and discussed the recent events.

Tom suggested I call Carol at Chateau Chic and cancel my appointment with her, especially in light of what had happened with the threatening phone call. I agreed and used Tom's cell phone to call her at the shop. Her assistant answered the phone and informed me Carol was not there and asked if he could take a message. I asked him to explain to her I was sorry but I would have to cancel our appointment due to a personal matter that required my attention. He said he would give Carol the message.

Now that my appointment was cancelled I was in no hurry to leave Tom's and he sensed I didn't want to be alone. "Listen Lizzie, here's the situation. I won't have a replacement car until the end of the week. You're dreading the thought of going home and being by yourself, which I completely understand. I hope you don't think I'm being presumptuous, but wouldn't it make sense for me to stay at your house for a few days or so, until I have a chance to try and find out more about that phone call? Besides, I'm supposed to take it a bit easy and you could be my nurse," he added with a wink, teasing me.

Actually, his plan made perfect sense and he got no argument from me. "Yes, that makes perfect sense and I don't think you're presumptuous at all. I'm relieved you thought of it. I would love to have the company." Before I could take it back, I winked at him, immediately hoping he did not think I was really being a tease. He laughed though, knowing I was joking, and I knew I could be myself with him and felt comfortable.

Tom packed some clothing and necessities and we drove back to Eureka, stopped at a local winery and market and picked up two bottles of wine, some fresh vegetables, chicken, steaks, and a loaf of French bread. Tom told me he liked to cook, which definitely impressed me. Before heading home, Tom asked me to drive by the decorating shop so he could see where it was located. Two cars were parked in front of the shop. Tom wrote down both license plate numbers. "I'll run a check on these after we get back to your house. When there are no obvious suspects you have to start to rule people out."

By the time we got back to my house it was late afternoon and the sun was a giant orange ball that would soon fall into the ocean. Tom took care of the alarm and groceries and poured two glasses of wine. "I think we both deserve a nice calm and uneventful evening, don't you?" as he handed me my glass.

"Yes, here's to a beautiful sunset and a nice, quiet evening." We clanged our glasses together in a toast. We went out on the back deck and watched the sun slowly lowering in the sky and then slide down into the ocean. It was a beautiful evening and a gentle breeze made the leaves rustle in the trees. It was quite a contrast to the previous evening when that awful thunderstorm had blown through. As I pointed out to Tom the tree that had been struck by lightning, he remarked that it was fortunate a serious fire had not started in the dry brush in the meadow out there.

We sat on the deck waiting for the sun to totally disappear into the sea. Tom pointed out Moonlight Cove, a beautiful slice of beach in the shape of the new moon that we could see from the terrace. "We should walk all the way down there sometime, maybe take a swim. It's supposed to be a really nice beach. Rumor has it that it's one of the most romantic spots in Northern California."

Further down the beach, at the end of the cove was Eureka Point and the lighthouse. The view was spectacular. The weather was nice so we decided to have dinner outside. Tom grilled steaks and vegetables and I went inside to the kitchen and prepared a salad. I got the plates and silverware, grabbed a bottle of wine, and put everything on a tray. I joined Tom outside and set the table.

We had a wonderful dinner and sat talking for quite awhile, finishing the bottle of wine. A giant waning moon rose in the sky, casting a silvery glow on everything. The gentle breeze caused the chimes hanging from the pergola to softly ring, the atmosphere was magical.

I was drawn to Tom for so many reasons. He was the only person I could trust and depend on. Luckily for me, he was a thoughtful and sensitive man as well as being strong and protective. Plus, he had such a wonderful sense of humor. I felt relaxed and secure with him being there and I enjoyed his company. The wine made me feel warm and mellow, and at that moment in time I was happy. Tom inquired, "A penny for your thoughts."

"I'm feeling relaxed for the first time in days and I'm enjoying the evening and your company." Actually, what I was thinking was that I was becoming very attracted to Tom but I wasn't quite ready to let him know. Still gun shy because of the recent events of my life, I held back. Then there was that nagging fact of reality, like a thorn in my side. I was still married.

"Great, then I would say we have succeeded in our mission for this evening. It's been quiet and calm and definitely enjoyable. I'm glad I'm here with you Lizzie."

"I'd be sitting in the kitchen by myself with a cell phone and a gun beside me on the table while I ate dinner alone. Doesn't that sound enjoyable? I'm glad you're here with me, Tom. I don't know what I'd do without you."

It started to get very cool after the sun went down so we went inside the house, cleaned up the dinner dishes, made some decaffeinated coffee and retired to the living room. Tom started a fire in the fireplace, lit some candles and put some music on. We sat on the floor in front of the fire drinking our coffee and watched sparks float up off the logs and listened to the fire crackle. An old romantic song came on the stereo and we both mentioned at the same time that it was one of our favorite songs.

"I learned to slow dance to this song in junior high," Tom said, as he stood up pulling me to my feet. "May I have this dance?" he asked with a smile.

"Of course, I'd be delighted."

Tom pulled me towards him and we danced closely until the song ended. He pushed some stray hair out of my face and gazed into my eyes. I felt as if I was under a spell, captivated by his charm. I gently touched the bandage on his forehead and asked him if it was painful.

"No, I feel fine, really good actually. Never better." He pulled me closer towards him and gently kissed me and said, "I have the feeling this is the beginning of a beautiful relationship." My heartbeat quickened and I felt giddy, like a teenager at a high school dance. I had always been a very thoughtful person, never jumping into a situation I was unsure of. Surprised by my own impulsiveness, I stood up on my toes and kissed Tom on his forehead right under the area that was bandaged. I wanted to kiss him again, on the mouth, but could not bring myself to be that forward. We stood there, very close for a minute, neither of us wanting the moment to end. I was falling for him and it seemed to me that the feeling was mutual.

## Chapter Eight

EUREKA POINT, CALIFORNIA

It was getting late and I was tired. Tom had brought his laptop with him from home saying he had some investigative work to do. He thought it would be best if he slept downstairs on the sofa. I got him a blanket and pillow from the upstairs linen closet and helped him make up the sofa and hoped he would be comfortable sleeping on it. "Do you have everything you'll need for the night?"

"Almost," he replied with a suggestive grin and a glance in my direction. I smiled shyly then walked over to the sofa, leaning over to give him a kiss on the cheek and said good night. He looked at me so tenderly I thought I might melt, but I still felt I wasn't ready to let myself go.

"Good night Lizzie. Sleep well."

I climbed the stairs slowly, not really wanting to go upstairs alone. Craig had been a deceitful jerk and a poor excuse for a man, but even so, and as sick as it was, I was missing him. Or at least I was missing the man I'd thought he was before I knew the truth about him. Now I was depressed and so tired. I striped off my clothes and slid into bed, emotionally drained.

Even though I could barely keep my eyes open I decided to listen to a favorite CD, one of the few personal items I was able to bring with me when I fled my old life. It had been in my car along with my CD player, headphones, and a novel I was reading.

The CD brought back memories of good friends and great times. Then my mind drifted back to Tom. Maybe he was my knight in shining armor. I had to rely on him for my own safety, but I knew I was emotionally vulnerable and I was becoming attracted to him. Would it be wise for me to trust another man again so soon? What were my instincts telling me since I was now so perceptive? These questions I asked myself, but before I could answer them, I fell sound asleep.

I dreamed that a loud crashing noise had startled me awake. Craig found out where I was and had broken into the house. I was desperately trying to get away from him. It was dark and I could hardly see, just a little bit from the light of the moon coming in the windows. I ran into the living room and could barely make out the form of Tom lying on the floor. As I got closer I saw a dark pool of blood on the floor around his head. I could hear Craig getting close to me so I started to run again and tripped over one of Tom's legs. I landed next to him on the floor and Craig fell on top of me. He forcefully grabbed my arms, pinning me down, and laughed in my face.

"I told you I'd find you bitch. I'll tell you what I'm going do. I promised to cut you into pieces and send you back to McClintock, but I killed him yesterday. So I'll just strangle you instead and leave you two lovebirds lying here next to each other. Besides, I'll get more of a thrill strangling you. I'll do it nice and slow and watch the life just slip out of you a little at a time."

Craig ripped the collar of my blouse away from my neck and put his strong hands around me. I clawed and tried to kick but I had no leverage. Slowly I felt my life slipping away, but I refused to give in. Finally, freeing one of my hands I grabbed and clawed at Craig's hands around my neck and tried to rip them away. My head felt hot, swollen, and just as I was about to suffocate, I heard Tom yelling.

"Lizzie, wake up! You're having a nightmare." Tom was desperately trying to unravel the CD player headset cord that had wrapped around my neck.

Realizing that I had been dreaming, I stopped fighting to free myself. Tom was finally able to remove the cord from around my neck. I was terrified by what I had dreamed and by what almost happened. Tom, relieved I had not strangled myself, put his arms around me to comfort me. "My God, are you okay?" he asked.

"Yes, I think I'm okay," I replied, and I told him about my dream.

"You've been through a lot, one traumatic thing after the next. Try to relax. How about a glass of water and some deep breaths – but not at the same time – I don't want you choking on the water," Tom said, making me laugh. I finished the water as he sat beside me on the bed, making sure I really was okay, and then he tucked me back under the covers.

I felt foolish. "I bet you wish you never got this assignment. Almost the equivalent of babysitting, right?"

"Actually, being your bodyguard is the best assignment I've ever had and I couldn't be happier," was Tom's response. "My last assignment was an old Sicilian man who had given key information in the trial that helped to put away a Mafia godfather. He was seventy-five years old and complained about everything. He smoked cigars, spit tobacco on the floor and had this annoying smoker's cough. To top everything else off, he snored really loud. I think I got about five hours of sleep that month. No, this is a piece of cake dear. Angel food cake." As had become his habit, he managed to make me laugh again and I felt much better.

Tom said he was going back downstairs to continue investigating the background of Carol, the owner of Chateau Chic. "Her last name is Turner. Her maiden name was Layton. Does that name mean anything to you?"

It certainly did. Stunned, I explained. "Carol Layton was my roommate when we both attended the same design school about fifteen years ago in New York City. We shared an apartment for a couple of years. She was one of my bridesmaids when Craig and I got married.

"When I started my own decorating business, she got pissed off because I didn't want to go into business with her. We had different ideas and opinions about decorating and I didn't feel it would be a good partnership. I told her that, in a nice way, but she was angry about it and with me. She asked me if Craig knew about my decision and wondered how he could have anything to do with a bitch like me. Craig always liked Carol and would stick up for her no matter what. They were close friends. I often used to think they were a bit too close, at least for my comfort."

"What do you mean? Do you think they were having an affair?"

"Looking back now, knowing what I know, I would say that is a possibility."

"You said you didn't actually meet Carol when you were at Chateau Chic the other day, didn't you?" Tom asked.

"That's right. Her assistant told me she was out on a job and I gave him my name and cell phone number. She called me later that day."

"Didn't you recognize her voice when she called?"

"No, she was all stuffed up and apologized for sounding so bad, explaining that she had a cold."

"Hmmm," Tom looked perplexed. "Well, I'll do some further checking. It bothers me that she and her assistant are the only other people that had your cell phone number. Nothing for you to worry about right now, but don't make arrangements to talk to or meet with her any time soon. Does she have your address?"

"No," I replied.

Tom kissed me on the forehead and lingered for a moment, then told me to get some sleep. He quietly left the room and shut the door. I closed my eyes but my mind kept going over the events of the last few days. I started thinking about Craig traveling here to California so often. Could he and Carol possibly still be friends, or even lovers? I tossed and turned, unable to fall asleep. Frustrated, I got up and decided to take a nice steamy bath that would hopefully help me to relax.

I slipped into the steamy tub and lay back into the warm water, placing a rolled up towel behind my neck. I watched the steam rise out of the tub and tried to focus on the warmth of the water as it eased the tension out of my body. Finally, I started to feel less tense and my tight muscles relaxed. Suddenly my eyes opened, I thought I heard noises coming from downstairs. I lay there very still in the hot water, concentrating on the noise, trying to make out what it was. I could faintly hear what sounded like two men talking.

I quietly slipped out of the steamy tub and grabbed a bath towel, wrapping it around my body. I went over and stood near the top of the stairway and listened intently. I could barely hear a word or two every so often.

Then suddenly the one man's voice got loud and angry sounding. Determined to find out what was going on, I slowly made my way down the staircase and crept up the dark hall towards the living room. The pocket door to the living room was closed. I got as close as I could to the door and listened intently. I could hear two men arguing and then the one man said, "Keep her quiet or get rid of her."

My heart started to pound, I could not believe what I was hearing. I quietly started to creep away so I would not be discovered lurking outside the doors but stopped when I heard music then a woman talking about how clean she had gotten her kitchen floor. What I had been hearing that entire time had been the television.

Feeling very foolish, I turned to make my way down the dark hallway to go back upstairs when I heard the door fly open and quickly found myself pushed to the floor with a gun in my back.

"Tom!" I screamed. Tom, realizing it was me, slumped down on the floor next to me. After a minute or so when we had both calmed down I explained to Tom that I had heard voices and had come downstairs to try and find out what was going on. Tom said he had fallen asleep on the sofa and had left the T. V. on. He was looking at me curiously, with a sheepish smirk on his face, which made me feel a bit perturbed, especially after what had just happened. "What is so amusing?" I demanded to know.

"Well, let's see. It is almost four o'clock in the morning and we're sitting here on the hallway floor and you've got nothing on but a towel. I'm sorry, but that strikes me as a bit unusual, and to be honest, quite amusing, you have to admit."

I looked down at the towel all but barely hanging on me and I must have turned several shades of red. Luckily it was dark enough that Tom probably didn't notice my blushing face. I quickly stood up, pulling the towel tightly around myself.

"Don't worry Lizzie. I didn't really see too much except for where the moonlight is streaming in and casting a glow on your feet. By the way, you have lovely toes." Unable to remain serious any longer, I finally burst out laughing until I had tears in my eyes.

"By the way, what are you doing in a towel anyway?"

"Oh, I couldn't get back to sleep after I almost strangled myself, so I decided to take a hot bath."

"It's a good thing you didn't fall asleep in the tub and drown. So in a way I saved you, again." He quipped and we laughed some more.

We were both too keyed up to even think about trying to go back to sleep. I went upstairs and dressed. When I came back downstairs, I joined Tom who was making a pot of coffee the kitchen. We quietly sat at the kitchen table sipping our coffee and watched the sky as it got lighter and lighter, until the night turned into a beautiful sunny morning.

Tom took a shower and I straightened things up in the living room. Tom came back downstairs with a smile on his face and said he felt like a new man. He went into the kitchen and the aroma of eggs, toast, and bacon filled the air. I knew he was making a scrumptious breakfast. A rush of warm contentment overcame me. What woman can resist a man who cooks? Tom made a delicious breakfast. "Where did you learn to cook like that?"

"Oh, my mom was a chef. She taught me everything I know. I worked as a short order cook at a diner to help support myself when I was in college. I'm glad my cooking pleases you."

After breakfast we sat outside sipping tea under the pergola. The sun sparkled on the water below and the sky was cloudless. The surroundings were beautiful and I enjoyed Tom being there with me, but I still felt uneasy.

Tom suggested we take a drive to Bayside so he could pick up his mail. I enjoyed the scenery as we passed little farms and local wineries along the way. Tom took me to the lighthouse in Cliffport, near The Inn.

"I often come here when I need to unwind or clear my head. I thought it might help you do the same." We walked around the lighthouse grounds and then further out to the rocky edge. Suddenly, the surf blew up, sending sea spray right in my direction. Tom grabbed my hand, pulling me back and we fell down together on the sand, laughing. Our lighthearted escapade was just what I needed. Tom stood up and helped pull me to my feet. He pulled me just hard enough that I rushed into him and we almost fell down together again, which caused another round of laughter. We brushed the sand off our clothing and then stood for a minute, admiring the view.

"I've always enjoyed coming here. Sometimes I come here to clear my mind. I brought you here hoping it might help you to do the same. You coming into my life at this time is no accident." He was searching my face for a reaction. I gulped hard and was dumbstruck. I had never been with anyone but Craig and the only feeling I had for him now, after what he had done, was disgust. I looked seriously at Tom and told him how I felt.

"The moment we met I felt an instant connection, and definitely an attraction. I like being with you and I feel safe, even though I might be in danger. I have feelings for you, but I need to take things slow. Because of what Craig did to me I'm emotionally unstable. I feel the need to have some type of closure with him before I can let myself go."

"What if Craig isn't found, if you never really have closure? Are you going to let him ruin the rest of your life and the possibility to love and be loved? Hasn't he taken enough from you already? He stole several years of your past. Don't let him take the rest of your life away. I don't mean to be pushy, but I'm falling head over heels for you and I don't want to be left standing here, finally feeling love again and not being able to act on it." Tom stopped talking and was deep in thought. After a few moments he said, "I'm sorry. I'm supposed to be doing a job here, not pressuring you into a love affair. I was taken by surprise, that's all."

It occurred to me that I might lose Tom's affection if I started putting up a wall to hold back my feelings. I didn't want that to happen. I owed Craig absolutely nothing, except for maybe a kick in the ass. It was time I wised up and stopped holding myself back. I grabbed Tom's hand and said, "No, don't be sorry, you weren't pushing me into anything. It's obvious that you have my best interests at heart." I stood up on my toes trying to reach my mouth to his. He was playing it cool purposely and just looked at me, not budging, until he could no longer contain himself, at which point he broke into a smile and said, "Yes," like he had won a contest, pulled me close to him and kissed me passionately.

After we kissed, I held onto Tom. "You were right about this place. It did help to clear my mind." We walked back to the car holding hands, got in and drove over to Bayside. We were on the road in front of Tom's cottage but he drove right past it, not even slowing down. I asked him what he was doing and he told me he thought he had seen someone near the back of his house. We drove further up the road and Tom parked. He told me to stay locked in the car while he went on foot to try to find out who was lurking around his house. He gave me his cell phone and told me to call the police if he didn't return in fifteen minutes.

Feeling uneasy, I kept Tom's cell phone in my hand and strained my neck trying to see back down the road. After several minutes had passed I saw a figure coming up the road. As the figure continued to get closer I was able to determine it was a man but I couldn't tell for sure if it was Tom. *It had to be, didn't it?*

Closer and closer the man continued to approach the car. As the man got close enough for me to see distinguish his features, I could tell it wasn't Tom. The man was very tall and was walking quickly. As he got even closer I could see that he had dark hair, was very well built, like a wrestler, and appeared to be Hispanic. I thought the worst and decided to push the seat back as far as it would go and crouched down as much as I could on the floor. My mind raced. The doors were locked and the car was parked far enough off the road that the man would probably not be close enough as he walked by to see me inside, I hoped. *Should I call the police?*

My thoughts were suddenly interrupted as I heard the sound of footsteps that stopped right outside the passenger door. I was so panic-stricken I fumbled and the cell phone, it slipped from my fingers and slid under the seat. I heard the lever of the door handle moving as the man tried to open the door. I desperately searched and felt around under my seat for the cell phone. I had just gotten my fingers on it when a crashing blow to the window above me made the glass shatter and pour down over me. A rock flew in and hit me in the head. Blood streamed into my eyes.

The last thought I had before I passed out was dancing with Tom.

# Chapter Nine

BAYSIDE, CALIFORNIA

The metallic taste of blood and the choking that followed brought me out of the temporary darkness of unconsciousness. Desperately, I frantically searched for the cell phone that had slipped from my hand again when I had been struck in the head. Through the narrow slits of my slightly opened eyes I could see the bright light of the sun and realized I was lying on my back and I heard voices above me.

Upon opening my eyes completely, I saw Tom hovering over me, with a look of extreme concern on his face. My head was throbbing badly, and not knowing the extent of my injury, I wondered if I might die. Tom stood close beside me and was telling me I would be okay. I was lifted up into an ambulance. Tom stayed with me and sat intently beside me.

"It's good she has regained consciousness," a woman attendant was telling him. "She has a bad contusion, a lot of lacerations from the glass and is in shock, but her vital signs are good." Tom grabbed my hand and held it tightly in his. I tried to ask him about the Hispanic man and find out what happened but the attendant told me to be quiet and rest, so I did.

When we got to the hospital emergency room the same doctor who had stitched up my cut hand after the car accident now cleaned up my face. My cuts were superficial but the contusion on the side of my head was very sore. A CT scan revealed no brain trauma. It took several minutes for a nurse to clean the blood off the wound and bandage it. I heard Tom speaking with a man outside my cubicle. The nurse told them it was okay for them to see me.

"Lizzie, this is Sergeant Thompson and he would like to ask you some questions, if you're up to it." The policeman asked me what had happened and I told him everything I could remember, up to the point when I had passed out. Then Tom finished the story for us both.

Tom was walking back to the car after finding evidence someone had tried to break into his cottage. As he approached the car he saw a tall Hispanic man slamming a large rock against the passenger side window of the car. Tom yelled for the man to stop and identified himself as a FBI agent. The man ran off, down an embankment, and into a wooded area. Tom ran after him but could not find him. Because he was concerned about me, he quickly returned to where the car was. When he got back to the car he found me crouched down and unconscious on the floor of the car and I looked to be in serious shape. He was able to unlock the car door by putting his hand in through the broken window. He found his cell phone on the floor near me and called nine-one-one.

The sergeant asked Tom if the man who threw the rock at the car was the same man he had seen lurking near the back of his house. Tom told him he wasn't sure because he hadn't gotten a good look at the man when we drove by.

Satisfied with what he had been told, Sergeant Thompson thanked us and offered us a ride home. Tom contacted my insurance company and arranged for the car to be towed to the auto repair shop.

The doctor gave me an antibiotic to take for five days, to make sure my wound would not become infected, and I was released. When I stood up my legs were weak and I realized how really stressed and physically drained I was. Sergeant Thompson drove us to my house and realized I was the woman McClintock had arranged for the local police force to keep an eye on. He told me to take it easy and promised me the local force was patrolling the area and would continue to do so.

Tom helped me into the house and took me into the living room. After helping me onto the sofa, he lovingly covered me with a blanket and lit a fire in the fireplace. He made a pot of tea and a snack of French bread and cheese. The fire felt warm and comforting. Tom sat on the floor next to the sofa and stroked my hair; I soon drifted off to sleep.

I slept like a baby and did not wake up until early the following morning. Still feeling groggy, I didn't open my eyes at first and let my mind wander. I could hear Tom on the phone in the kitchen talking to someone about my car. I loved the sound of his voice. He had a calming effect on me.

Slowly sitting up, I thought about my mother and wondered what she would think about the situation I found myself in. She would probably tell me to focus on the positive. I admired my mother for her understanding and wisdom and I missed my parents very much. The only positive I could find in my situation was Tom. Plus, I really liked this house and Eureka Point. Maybe everything had happened for a reason. No, I wasn't going to get weak and give up. I promised McClintock I would stay strong and that's what I would do.

Tom walked into the living room with a smile on his face. "Well, if it's not sleeping beauty. I have some good news for you. Sergeant Thompson just called to tell me that a man who fits the description of the one who tried to break into your car was found and arrested last night on a felony drug charge. He's in jail and bail has been denied. Your car will be finished tomorrow and my new replacement car will be here later this morning. It's about time some things started going our way."

I managed a smile but my head was throbbing. Tom could sense my discomfort. "Lizzie, lie back down and take it easy today, doctor's orders. He told me you would probably feel very tired for a day or so and I'm supposed to make sure you get lots of rest. Are you ready for breakfast? You should eat and take your antibiotic."

"Okay," I said, although I really was not very hungry.

Tom turned the TV on, handed me the remote control and walked out to the kitchen singing, "I left my heart in San Francisco." His jovial mood made me feel secure. After all, if he was feeling that things were improving and there was a reason to be happy, I should too.

A morning news show was on and I was half listening to the announcer giving her account of the national news when my husband's name was mentioned. I turned up the volume and paid close attention.

"Tom, there's something about Craig on the news, come quick."

Tom stood beside me and we both listened intently. Craig's picture appeared on the screen. The photo was from several years ago, when he still looked young and innocent. The announcer said, "Craig Montgomery, the New York based entrepreneur and gourmet guru, who was thought to have fled to South America after being sought by the FBI for drug smuggling and related charges, is believed to be in the San Francisco area. His private plane was found in an isolated field near El Pacifico, approximately thirty-five miles north of San Francisco. The plane was discovered in good condition and it is assumed that Mr. Montgomery safely landed the plane. The fugitive is also an amateur off-road motorcyclist who has been known to fly to remote locations, cycle to desolate areas, and camp in the wilderness for long periods of time. His wife, interior designer Katie O'Hara, is also missing. Craig Montgomery is considered to be armed and dangerous. Anyone with information concerning him should contact the FBI immediately."

I sat on the sofa in total shock and dismay and didn't say a word for several minutes. Tom sat close beside me, pondering the situation then called McClintock. After conversing for awhile, it was decided that Tom and I would drive further north to an FBI safe house and stay there, at least until the FBI could locate Craig and bring him into custody.

Tom went upstairs with me and helped me pack my things. He told me to make sure I took some warm clothing and a jacket. Feeling stressed and anxious I hurried. We went back downstairs. As Tom got his things together, he explained that FBI agents in two different cars were on their way. They would leave one car in the driveway for us to take. We would have to drive over to Tom's cottage so he could pick up some things he would need to take along.

The agents showed up a few moments later. Tom's demeanor had become very serious and I knew he was concerned about this latest development. The agents spoke to Tom briefly and I sensed the need for urgency. We had to leave immediately. In just a few minutes we were pulling up in front of Tom's cottage and we both quickly got out of the car and went inside. Tom grabbed a bag he had already packed for just such a situation as the one we were in. Once again, we were on our way.

Tom drove and I sat quietly, my mind spinning. I asked myself how Craig could have found out where I was living. Could it be a coincidence that he had come to Northern California? Suddenly, something occurred to me. Craig and Carol knew each other and it was not out of the realm of possibility that they were having an affair. Maybe Craig had taken all those business trips to California to be with her. Was it possible that Craig was in Northern California to see Carol? Maybe he had no idea I was in this area. I told Tom what I was thinking.

"Well, that is certainly a possibility." Tom contacted his office and told them to keep an eye on Carol in case Craig contacted her. Good thinking Lizzie! You may have a future in investigation. I think we would make a good team, don't you?"

"Oh yes, I can see it now: Owens and Harrison – Private Investigators." And I smiled for the first time that day.

We were heading northeast and away from the coastline. The terrain became more wooded and mountainous. Tom told me we would be going to a secluded safe house, which was really a cabin, in an area named Cedar Rock. The afternoon sun was fading and with a sinking feeling in the pit of my stomach, I hoped we would be there soon.

Just as the sun was setting we pulled onto a dirt drive that winded up to a log cabin house off the main road. It looked rather nice, like a vacation home. We grabbed our bags, Tom unlocked the front metal security door that was faux painted to match the wood, and we went inside. There was, of course, a security system that Tom knew how to operate and had the code for. It was tied into the FBI communications system. Tom immediately contacted his office and told them about my theory of the possible Craig-Carol connection.

Tom showed me around the cabin and I knew it was safe and secure. All the windows were triple paned and bullet proof. The kitchen was fully stocked with non-perishable and canned goods, soda, coffee, tea, and frozen meals. Famished, I made a pot of canned chicken noodle soup. Tom reminded me to take my antibiotic.

Funny, with everything that was going on I had forgotten about my most recent incident until he mentioned it. I ran my fingers gently over my face feeling the cuts and scrapes. As I stopped to think about what had happened to me, the exhaustion I felt almost overwhelmed me. I finished my soup and went back to the great room where I snuggled up on the sofa. Tom lit a fire and thoughtfully covered me with a blanket.

Thinking about having to leave my new home because of Craig made me angry. I hoped this whole ordeal would be over soon so I could get on with my life. What would happen if Craig was found and put in prison? Would I then be safe to live my life or would the drug cartel still be after me? *Stop thinking*, I told myself. I would just have to wait and tough it out. At least Tom was with me and the cabin was warm and inviting. Tom was looking outside and chuckled as he announced that it had started to snow. I was feeling cold and drained and hated the thought of snow. I hoped it wouldn't amount to anything. As if Tom picked up on my negative feelings, he came over to sit down beside me. He put his arms around me and gently rocked me like a baby, kissing my head. I felt warm and secure, but sick and tired, all at the same time. Tom had developed the uncanny ability to read my mind and told me not to worry, that he would take care of me.

"When we were at the lighthouse, I told you I was falling for you. You mean a lot more to me than just some alias I've been assigned to protect, who I might get lucky with. I can't bear the thought of us going our separate ways when this is all over. I think we've come into each other's lives for a reason. I've been seriously thinking about things. Part of me was hoping that Craig would never be found, so you would have to stay here and I could protect you, forever. The other part of me has been hoping Craig will be caught and put away so you can be free to live your life in peace, but I was already hoping to be a part of that life.

"After my wife died, I really didn't think I could come to love another woman. Now you've come into my life and changed everything. I know you're tired and need to rest but I wanted to let you know how I feel about you. I love you." He touched my chin and turned my face in his direction. I was completely overwhelmed and exhausted. My head hurt and all I wanted to do was sleep.

I smiled at Tom and told him he was right. I did need to rest. I regretted the harsh way I had said that the moment the words left my lips. I should have been nicer about it and I hoped I had not hurt his feelings. My mind was so overloaded it would take time for me to slowly sort though my thoughts and feelings regarding my new life. One indisputable fact kept gnawing at me. No matter how much he disgusted me, I was still legally married to Craig.

Tom slowly got up and walked over to the window. He looked worried and confused. It hadn't been my intention to alienate him, just to be honest with him. I didn't want to lead him on when I was so emotionally confused. But I did care for him deeply. That I couldn't deny.

## Chapter Ten

CRAIG: WOODED HILLS OF NORTHERN CALIFORNIA

Craig was a man on a mission. Even though Katie was too straight-laced and certainly not adventurous enough for his liking, she was his wife after-all. Furious when he found out she had turned to the FBI, he decided he was going to find her if it was the last thing he did. A wife's duty was to support her husband, no matter what. She had married him. He didn't have to push her into it. He had given her everything a woman could want; a beautiful home, vacations several times a year, and he had even given her an allowance any woman would have found more than sufficient. As far as Katie knew he had even been faithful to her. With Carol living on the other side of the country where he would often travel on business, the arrangement worked out quite well. But now Katie had turned on him. She had a lot of nerve. But she wasn't going to get away with it. He would make sure of that.

When the federal authorities had uncovered Craig's drug ring he had taken some precautions. He knew they were onto him but he had not been sure just how much Katie actually knew. His bodyguard, Julio, a former professional wrestler, had been paid handsomely to follow his wife's every move and he had done just that, reporting her meeting with special agent McClintock. Craig knew all about the FBI's so-called protection program for witnesses and informants. Katie was seen going into FBI Headquarter in New York City with McClintock. He had inside information that they had changed Katie's appearance and identity and were sending her to the West Coast.

Craig's bodyguard waited at the airport terminal and sure enough McClintock appeared with Katie incognito. He knew it was Katie. His bodyguard had snapped a picture. It was definitely Katie's body, just different hair. His man was even able to get a ticket on the same flight to San Francisco staying right on her tail. He even managed to sit across the aisle from her on the plane.

When Craig was eleven years old his mother, a raving lunatic, had taken up with some California fitness guru and left Craig with his grandparents, his father's family, the Montgomery's. She said she would send for him after she got situated in California. She never did.

His father and mother had never married and Craig was not even one hundred percent positive that Stephen Montgomery was his real father. Stephen Montgomery lived with his parents on their estate and despised his son's presence. Craig's grandparents tolerated his presence but had showed him no real love or affection. But they provided him with expensive clothing, hobbies and things just to keep him quiet. In his mind he was unlovable because he was unloved.

Craig had learned to only let people see the person he wanted them to think he was. To get where and what he wanted in life he knew how to put on the charm. Katie had definitely fallen for his charm.

Craig's grandparents got tired of putting up with their grandson's expensive problems and kicked him out of their house when he was eighteen years old. He sponged off some friends for a while, until one of them made him angry. Having no further use for him, Craig slit his throat when he was sleeping. As a result, Craig was diagnosed to be bipolar with sociopath tendencies and was put on medication. He stopped taking the pills when he couldn't afford them; any money he earned was paying for cocaine, his medication of choice.

He was arrested for illegal weapons possession and found to be mentally incompetent and was put in a state mental institution. When he was released he decided to find another successful and wealthy family to latch onto.

He had read about Katie in the newspaper and decided he was going to have her. He found out as much as he could about her. He knew where she liked to dine and who her friends were. He even he planned how he would meet her. His plan worked and by the time Craig turned twenty-two, he and Katie were engaged. Six months later they were married. Katie's parents gave them a lavish wedding and a handsome amount of money that Craig had no problem getting Katie to hand over to him so he could start his own business. The business, after-all, would help them become successful. It would be a wise investment for their future.

Craig was not a fool. He knew how to work people and he really did have some talent and a good business sense. His businesses flourished and he became more and more successful. The problem was he became greedy. The more money he made, the more he wanted. He became intent on having as much money as he could and didn't care what he had to do to get it or who he hurt doing it.

So, when approached, he became involved with a South American based drug cartel. He was making millions of dollars a year. Everything was working out just right. The only glitch had been when Carol demanded more from him, threatening to tell Katie about their long-standing affair and his underworld connections. He worked out a plan for her too.

He offered her enough money to start her own decorating business but she would have to do it on the other side of the country. She agreed. Craig continued to support her and to continue their affair, traveling to California "on business" several times a month. Things went smoothly for several years until some nosey FBI drug enforcement investigator discovered Craig's drug operation.

Dirt-biking his way around the rocky terrain near the wooded hills in Northern California was nothing new to Craig. He had done so by choice many times before. But he was not thrilled with this weather. The wet snow kept flying onto his helmet visor and he had to stop every few minutes to wipe it off. The digital GPS tracking device attached to his wrist showed him exactly where his wife and that FBI agent who was with her were located. Carol, pain in the ass that she was, had done well. Katie had done exactly as they thought she would. She hadn't been in Eureka even a week and was lured to Carol's decorating shop. They had no trouble getting her cell phone number, but were unable to track her with it. But they figured that the FBI agent's cell phone was probably set up with GPS and could be digitally tracked if they could just get his number.

With a little ingenuity, they were able to scare Katie into not using her cell phone by calling and threatening her. Then she would call Carol at Chateau Chic from Tom's cell phone. They would be able to get Tom's cell phone number when she called Carol using his phone, and then digitally track their location. The threatening phone call would also scare Katie, who would probably not want to be alone and she would ask Tom to stay with her. So wherever Tom and his cell phone were, Katie would be there too. Craig could take them both out at the same time. Craig just hoped the FBI would not move Katie again before he could find her.

He drove on through the dark and dismal night. He could almost taste revenge. The closer he got the more excited he became at the thought of what he would do to them both. Assuming they were locked up in some secure building did not discourage Craig. Actually, it would make it more interesting. Like a hunter, he would patiently wait for his prey to come out into the open, into clear sight. They would have to come out eventually. He would simply watch and wait.

Through the driving wet snow Craig could barely make out the yellow window light far in the distance. As he rode closer, the light got bigger and brighter. A minute later he could smell the smoke from their fireplace. He decided to turn the cycle off, as to not alarm anyone that he was in the area. He then got his gear together and went the rest of the way on foot.

When he was satisfied he was close enough to spy on them, Craig found an area where he could set up a temporary shelter hidden from view. He had enough rations to get him through a week or two if need be, but he doubted it would take that long. Under his camouflaged tarp Craig set up his gear and watched. Soon the lights were turned off and he assumed they had gone to bed. Wanting to make it impossible for them to make a quick get-away, Craig formulated a plan of attack. He would first have to steal their vehicle. If they tried to get away on foot, they wouldn't have a chance in hell.

## Chapter Eleven

TOM: CEDAR ROCK, CALIFORNIA

I stood up and walked over to the window, staring into the darkness. I hoped Lizzie's cold response was due to exhaustion and her recent ordeal rather than a reaction to my profession of love for her. I could see nothing except the wet snow driving down and dissolving as soon as it hit the ground. It was a miserable night. I thought I heard something in the distance. Listening intently I was sure I faintly heard the high-pitched wine of an engine. Lizzie must have noticed the look of intent concentration on my face and asked me if something was wrong.

"Shh...I thought I heard something." Yes, I was sure of it now. I heard the sound of a motorcycle or all-terrain vehicle in the distance.

Suddenly, it stopped. My mind raced as I remembered the news reporter had said Craig would often fly to a location, land and then use a dirt bike to travel to remote areas. But how could he know where we were? My analytical mind kept searching for an answer. Then it came to me.

It had to be my cell phone. Craig was a resourceful man with underworld connections and probably had access to a GPS positioning scanner enabling him to digitally track through my cell phone, which had a tracking device. Craig would have to know my cell phone number, which he could have gotten from Carol, if she was in on this scheme. If it was Craig out there he already knew where we were.

"Lizzie, turn off the lights," I said urgently. Quickly, I explained my theory to her. It was possible there might be someone else in the area, perhaps campers, but I doubted it, not in this weather. I had to make a decision, come up with a plan. We could not just stay there and do nothing. After weighing our limited options, I made a decision. We should get out of there as quickly as possible. I contacted my office, advising them I thought Craig was in the area, and told them we would be leaving the cabin to drive to the nearest town. My contact would alert the local authorities immediately to let them know Craig was probably in the area near the cabin.

As we quickly gathered our things together we both suddenly stopped, realizing we heard what sounded like our car, which had been parked in front of the cabin, being driven away. By the time I got to the front window I could barely see the red taillights through the driving wet snow. At least I knew which direction Craig had gone. There was a Jeep in the shack behind the cabin that we could use to get away. I had learned through experience it was always better not to remain somewhere if the enemy knew you were there.

"Lizzie, I'm going to go get the Jeep in the shack behind the cabin. Grab our stuff and be ready to jump in but keep the front door locked and don't come out until you see me in the jeep out front." I pulled the gun out of my holster and quickly went out the door, into the darkness.

Making my way to the shack through the driving rain and snow was difficult. I cupped my left hand over my eyes shielding them from the rain and held the slippery wet gun in my other hand. Finally, I made it to the shack and jumped into the old, well-used Jeep.

Not wanting to be seen, I intentionally did not turn on the headlights. Driving in poor visibility with no lights made the trip from the shack to the cabin seem unbearably endless. As soon as I made it to the front of the cabin Lizzie was out the door and quickly jumping into the Jeep. I whispered to her to be quiet. Slowly, we crept down the winding dirt road. Almost at the bottom, I slammed on the brakes. Headlights were beaming up the road at us, unmoving.

"Get down," I whispered. Time seemed to stand still as I forced myself to concentrate while adrenaline pumped through my veins. My breathing became short and tense as I waited for something to happen.

Suddenly, out of the wooded darkness, not from the direction of the lights, but from my side of the Jeep, Craig jumped out, pointing a rifle directly at us. With the added bow and arrow quiver on his back, he looked like a crazed madman.

He laughed uncontrollably like a raving lunatic.

I knew the agent would send the local police to the area to try to find Craig. My cell phone would pinpoint our exact location for him. I just hoped the authorities would get there in time.

"Don't worry your little head about your boyfriend. I'm not going to shoot him, yet," Craig seethed. "He's used to being hunted so it's only right that I chase him down like a wild animal and put an arrow right through his heart."

I could see that Lizzie was terrified, that she was forcing herself to appear calm. She looked directly at Craig and said, "I was wondering when you'd finally find us and rescue me. Why didn't you take me with you? They came to me Craig, and told me that the South American drug cartel was after me. I did what I had to do to stay alive, so I could find you darling. God how I missed you!

"Craig honey, they're on your trail. Don't complicate things by adding murder to your problems. Let's just get out of here, together. We can fly to Aruba or Costa Rica and live anonymously. I have lots of money stashed away in a Swiss bank account. We could live like royalty."

"Well, let's talk about this Katie, you lying bitch! If you're telling me the truth about having money in a Swiss bank account that means you've been holding out on me all this time. If it's not true, then it means you're lying to me now just to save your own ass and maybe keep Romeo here alive. So you could have your cake and eat it too. I don't think so."

Craig demanded that I get out of the Jeep and put my hands up. Below the level of the side window of the Jeep, out of Craig's view, I held my gun. Not looking at her, I put the gun in Lizzie's hand, slowly opened the door, put my hands up, and got out. Craig ordered me to turn around and walk backward over to him. I stumbled over rocks and branches but slowly made my way over to where Craig was waiting. I hoped Lizzie would realize the only way we might possibly survive was if she would be able to shoot Craig. I looked at her, and looked down where she held the gun, and gave a slight backward nod in Craig's direction. I looked at Lizzie one last time, and silently formed the words *shoot him*, then *I love you*.

Just as I got within a few feet of Craig, I heard him move, and saw the butt of his rifle coming at me. I tried to jump out of the way and was able to avoid the brunt of the assault. The butt of the rifle grazed the injured area of my forehead, causing me to temporarily lose consciousness and fall to the ground. Dazed, I desperately tried to focus and get on my feet.

Lizzie shrieked in horror. Craig laughed hideously like a madman and screamed for her to get out of the Jeep.

Still in a daze, I watched Lizzie as she slowly opened her door and get out of the Jeep. Craig leaped at her like a leopard after prey. She pointed the gun at Craig when suddenly a gunshot rang out from over in the trees hitting Craig in the side of the head. His head swung grotesquely sideways and his body slammed onto the sopping ground, dead weight. Lizzie turned away from the sight of him and fell, retching onto the wet grass.

The skies opened, now pouring cold rain, it slapped me in the face and brought me out of my semi-conscious state and back to reality. I finally managed to make my way over to where Lizzie was laying on the ground. Not knowing who had fired the shot that killed Craig, I quickly laid on top of Lizzie, shielding her. The Sheriff ran out of the trees and yelled to us, identifying himself. As Lizzie sobbed uncontrollably, I held her tightly in my arms. "It's over now. It's all over."

The Sheriff quickly made his way over to us, realized we needed medical attention and called for medics to meet us at the cabin. The Sheriff assisted us into the Jeep and drove us back to the cabin. He helped us inside just as the medics arrived. They covered Lizzie with a dry, warm blanket and checked my head injury. Before leaving, the medics advised me to help Lizzie out of her wet clothing and to keep her warm.

"Lizzie, sweetheart, we have to get you out of those wet clothes. I'll be right back." I ran out to the Jeep to get our bags so we would have a change of clothing.

Sheriff Stevens was right outside and took a brief statement from me. He said he would take care of everything then asked for both of us to come into town the following morning to give him our full statements so he could wrap things up. I thanked him again and agreed that we would come to the station the following morning.

When I returned to the cabin Lizzie was standing in front of the fireplace, stripped down to her underwear. Appearing, as if in a trance, she was drying herself with a towel. Her wet skin glowed as the firelight danced upon her flesh.

I stood behind her and she slowly turned to face me. Her eyes sparkled with firelight, silently calling me to her. Without saying a word, I took the towel and slowly went over the curves of her body, drying the wet drops as they fell from her drenched hair onto her shoulders and then slid further down, onto the rounded tops of her full breasts. Our eyes met, finally knowing Craig was no longer a threat, relieved we did not have to run and hide, and unable to hold back any longer, our passion ignited.

Lizzie pulled at my wet shirt, unable to remove it fast enough. I tore off my wet clothing as Lizzie removed the remainder of hers. I stood close, taking in the sweet, hypnotic scent of her, captivated by her beauty. "God, you're beautiful," I said, breathing heavily in her ear. I grabbed her to me and we fell onto the rug in front of the fireplace in each other's arms.

My heart was pounding so hard I thought Lizzie could probably hear it but I didn't care. She finally let herself go. All that mattered was what we felt at that moment in time. We had been attracted to each other from the moment we first met, had felt an instant connection. Those feelings, which had been held back, now came loose.

Passionately, we kissed until we were unable to hold back any longer. Lizzie finally let the walls she had been confined behind come tumbling down. As I laid flat on my back, Lizzie lightly brushed her fingertips along my damp skin. I shivered then sighed deeply as currents of pleasure raced through me.

She started to kiss my body, up one side and down the other. I felt as if I was on fire and pulled her to me. Surrendering completely, she came down on me and passionately we made love.

I no longer questioned her feelings for me. I could feel her love from the look in her eyes and from the moans of passion that came from deep within her. In a low throaty voice she whispered in my ear, "I love you Tom." I had longed to hear her say those words. This would be a second chance at love for both of us and the memory of this moment in time would stay with us forever. It was, without question, the most romantic and sensual experience either of us had ever experienced.

Afterwards, as Lizzie lay in my arms, we looked into each other's eyes and it felt as if we could see each other's souls. She remained lying in my arms on the rug in front of the fireplace. The fire now diminished to mere glowing embers and the room in darkness, a silvery beam of moonlight streamed in the window and cast a glow upon us. The rain stopped and the clouds parted like a curtain opening on the enormous moon that glowed in the sky like a golden orb suspended from the Heavens. And at that moment in time no words needed to be spoken. We felt that destiny had brought us together and everything was as it should be.

# Chapter Twelve

KATE, EUREKA POINT, CALIFORNIA

What an absolutely magical and gorgeous night it was. Mesmerized by the pure mystical beauty of the new moon, I took a deep breath of sweet air as the gentle breeze made the chimes hanging in the Banyan tree tingle softly. I thought back to the night I had viewed the moon from my dining room window as I ate dinner alone, my heart aching, feeling insignificant and unloved. I was amazed at how drastically things had changed for the better.

As I gazed into my kitchen window I could see the silhouettes of my parents in the yellow light and heard them laughing lightheartedly, undoubtedly at some joke or funny story that Tom had told them. Trying to take it all in I felt giddy and so alive, my heart full of love. Like a child on Christmas morning, I was excited and happy. Things had indeed worked out for the best. I felt so extremely lucky.

Tom, with two glasses of wine in his hands, came out of the kitchen door and sauntered over to me. Handing me a glass he gestured a toast in my direction and said jovially, "Here's to you Katie O'Hara. Your Irish eyes are twinkling with starlight and never have you looked so beautiful sweetheart." Just then my mother opened the kitchen door and said good night, then added sweetly, "Tom dear, thanks for taking care of our Katie."

It had been almost three months since that unbelievable night when Craig had been killed. I had been broken-hearted by the manner of his death. More so by the tragedy of the life he had lived. As soon as I got over the initial shock of what had happened and Tom had been notified that the cartel had been taken down, I contacted my parents and friends. I explained everything to them and asked Mom and Dad to come visit and stay with me for a while. I had very little problem deciding where my home would be, now that I could be myself again.

Carol had been arrested on conspiracy charges because of her knowledge of Craig's involvement with the drug cartel and her involvement in his plan to find me and do me harm. In a way I felt sorry for her. She was another person badly affected by Craig's evil ways. But she had been conniving and selfish. I guess she got what she deserved. In searching Craig's plane, information was found by the FBI that helped them to find the head of the drug cartel he had been involved with. I was now safe and free to live my life as I wished. I could have gone home to New York, to get things in order there, but I decided to wait. I had much more important things to take care of. My first priority was my happiness and the love Tom and I had been so lucky to find in each other.

Tom and I had spent the first few weeks just getting to know each other better and we both knew our instincts had been correct all along. The only thing that was undecided was what Tom would call me, Lizzie or Katie. With his unique sense of humor, he ended up calling me both, at different times. But then had decided he liked the sound of Katherine Elizabeth O'Hara and called me Kate. Tom had shown me his true colors right from the beginning.

He had suffered some memory loss due to brain trauma from the two blows to his head; the first from the car accident and then again when Craig had hit him with his rifle. He was on disability from work and we were making the most of the free time we had. Soon we would be taking a cruise for some well-deserved rest, relaxation, and most definitely, romance. Like two young lovers, we couldn't get enough of each other.

I looked up to find Tom peering at me with a puppy-dog-like look on his face. Taking the glass out of my hand and putting it down on the patio table, he put his arm around me, and with his hand gently pressing on my back, brought me close to him. He put his other hand on my face and gently caressed the outline of my jaw and chin. Looking into my eyes, he smiled and kissed me tenderly. Almost melting in the emotion of the moment, I responded and we kissed passionately.

"I love you Kate"; he spoke softly in my ear. I grabbed the back of his neck with my hand and cuddled his face.

"I love you too," and we kissed again. We then walked hand in hand to the edge of the hill that overlooked the ocean and stood watching the sliver of moonlight glimmer on the water. A shooting star streaked across the sky and I told Tom to make a wish.

Tom sweetly replied, "My wish already came true."

# *The End*

To find out more about Betty Ann Harris and her awesome books you can go to:

http://www.eurekapoint.blogspot.com/

A little peek into Betty's world!

As a reader and writer who loves a good mystery to solve and I always guess the "who did it?" right. I'm a wife and mom and I work from home.

Made in the USA